Helena Brett's Career

by

Desmond Coke

Helena Brett's Career
by Desmond Coke

Copyright © 2024

All Rights reserved.

ISBN: 978-93-62205-46-9

Published by

DOUBLE 9 BOOKS

2/13-B, Ansari Road
Daryaganj, New Delhi – 110002
info@double9books.com
www.double9books.com
Tel. 011-40042856

This book is under public domain

ABOUT THE AUTHOR

Desmond Coke, an esteemed author renowned for his insightful storytelling and profound exploration of human ambition, leaves an indelible mark with his masterpiece "Helena Brett's Career." Set against the backdrop of the bustling cityscape of London in the late 19th century, Coke's novel intricately weaves a narrative that follows the journey of the ambitious protagonist, Helena Brett, as she navigates the challenges and triumphs of pursuing her career aspirations in a male-dominated society. Coke's vivid prose and meticulous attention to detail bring Helena's world to life, capturing the essence of Victorian-era London with authenticity and depth. Through Helena's trials and tribulations, Coke delves into themes of ambition, determination, and the pursuit of success, offering readers a poignant reflection on the complexities of womanhood and the evolving role of women in society. "Helena Brett's Career" stands as a timeless classic of literature, celebrated for its compelling characters, richly drawn settings, and thought-provoking exploration of societal norms and expectations. With its engaging storyline and profound insights, Coke's novel continues to captivate readers, leaving a lasting impression on all who embark on Helena's journey of self-discovery and empowerment.

CONTENTS

PART III
HELENA BRETT'S CAREER

PART I
HOW IT HAPPENED

CHAPTER I
ADVICE

"Of course," said Kenneth Boyd, with the abrupt conviction of one whose argument is off the point at issue, "it's absolutely obvious. You ought to marry."

The man who ought to marry was no more pleased to hear it than most of his kind. He scowled angrily: then smiled, as though contempt were a more fit reply. He was tall, broad, firm-looking, with smooth dark hair still low upon his forehead, and certainly looked in no need of drastic remedies.

He knocked his pipe out on the grate before he answered, but when the words came, they burst forth like an explosion.

"You married men," he cried, turning the attack, "are just like parrots. You can only say one thing. You're worse than parrots: you're gramophones—or parrots with a gramophone inside. You're always saying one thing, 'Marry!' and you say it jolly long. I honestly believe you've got a Trades Union, unless it's merely nasty feeling! That probably is it. You hate to see others as happy as you used to be!"

Whereat, comforted, he stretched his long legs and lay back on the deep chair in a better humour.

"No," said the other gently. "We hate to see them miserable and know they'll never realise man's one chance of happiness till it's too late."

He spoke in very earnest tones and looked almost anxiously across at his friend, now quite happy again with the flushed sensation of having achieved something at any rate not too far from an epigram. A peaceful smile played round the big mouth which alone betrayed weakness in his pale, clear-cut face.

How young he was in some ways, Kenneth Boyd reflected—in self-complacency, for one! And yet, in others, how much too settled and fixed for his years. Here he was, a ten-year resident of these rooms—comfortable enough, yes—looked after by a sister; turning out his yearly novel, no worse but no better than the one before; an old bachelor at thirty-five, and yet too young to speak of marriage as anything except a rather tasteless joke!

He watched him anxiously, as he might watch his patients at the hospital, and wondered whether he was beyond helping.

Hubert Brett said nothing. He was angry.

Why, he was wondering, had he telephoned for Boyd to come along at all? He always *had* asked Boyd, of course, even in the dear old Oxford days, when he was in a difficulty. Boyd's great forehead, thick chin, and deep voice gave him a sort of solid, comfortable air: and he was never sympathetic.... Probably his medical work—it was not nice, quite, to think of it like that—made him a restful person to consult? He always smoothed you down and made you feel that what you meant to do would be entirely for the best.

But he had been off form to-night....

Marry, indeed! Why, that had nothing to do with the case at all. It was Ruth's maddening stupidity that had made him ask Kenneth in. These rows with one's sister were horrible—and bad for work.... Besides, they used to be such pals as kids: it wasn't nice, now, to be quarrelling like any
• costermonger and his wife. Yet each absurd quarrel was followed by one more absurd.

What had it been all about to-night? He had forgotten that already. The actual row was a surprise. Ruth had started this one. He had not seen it coming, even, till they were both on their feet.

She was so maddening, you see!

He didn't mind an egoist. He sometimes thought, in moments of depression, he was one himself (but he did not believe in introspection). It was an egoist who claimed to be a martyr that aroused his anger.

Ruth was always claiming to have sacrificed herself. *She* didn't matter. No one must consider her. She hadn't married. She gave her life up willingly to her dear brother. If he trod on her sometimes, she only liked to feel that he was free to wing his way to fame. And all that sort of stuff ... when all the while, she never did a single thing he wanted, but in the most selfish way made everything as hard as it could be for his work, when she herself was doing nothing! What a fuss if he was half an hour or so late for their lonely meal! How could it matter? He was in the middle of a paragraph, sometimes: and what did she do after dinner, anyhow? Nothing but play Patience, while he went back to work! How could it make any difference at what hour she dined?...

Probably to-night had been some trifle of that sort: he had forgotten, really; but at the end of it she had stood up and said, for the first time: "Well, I can always be turned out. There's no real reason why we should live together."

"The first sensible remark you've made," he had replied, made elementary by anger, and gone out to telephone to Boyd.

Why, after all, *did* they live together? Would he be happier without her? Or would a cook-housekeeper be worse? How did other men get on? Most of them, somehow, seemed to marry.... Boyd would know, though—he went to so many homes. But Boyd might say that it was not quite fair on Ruth.... That was nonsense, though. Brothers weren't ever meant or bound to keep their sisters, and thirty-eight was not too old for women to get married. It was the fashionable age. Nobody now cared for girls. Only Ruth never wanted to go out, or, if she did, it was to some quite silly show where he could not be seen.... Well, he would see what Boyd said. That was the best way.

And Boyd, having listened to the passionate recital in an owlish silence, had answered: "It's quite obvious. You ought to marry!" Just what those idiots of doctors always said. Marriage and golf were their only two ideas, even for any one with liver.

"*Why* ought I to marry?" he blazed out suddenly, to the surprise of his friend, who could not follow his thought during the long pause.

"Why, my dear fellow? Because you're stagnating—because it is life's second stage—because you've got beyond the first—because each of your books is exactly like the last——"

This ceased to be theory. Hubert was in arms at once.

"I don't see that," he said in a hard voice, almost sulkily. "As a matter of fact, several of the critics went out of their way to call *The Bread of Idleness* new, original, etcetera."

"Yes," replied Kenneth Boyd, who secretly enjoyed wounding just deeply enough his friend's self-esteem; "the plot was different, but its heroine the same. You had her in *Wandering Stars*; you had her in *Life*; you've had her in them all. There is a Hubert Brett type no less than a Gibson Girl."

"I still don't see, even so," Hubert icily replied, "exactly why I have to marry."

Kenneth Boyd smiled unseen. "Because to widen your art, you must widen your idea of woman. If you really know one woman, they say, then you can know them all."

A good deal of the author's self-esteem returned. He looked relieved. So that was all, was it?

"If you know them all, as I do, by study," he answered, "you don't *want* to know one."

And now indeed Kenneth Boyd peered at him seriously, as at a patient very critical.

"That sort of remark," he said, "just shows that you know nothing about women and ought to marry one."

Hubert laughed. "Dear old Kenneth!" and there was pity in his voice. "Perhaps I should, if I knew nothing of them really. But I'm afraid I know too much."

His counsellor made no reply. He always knew when he had failed. He also knew, from long experience, the only weapon that availed when once the hard line came round Brett's weak lips. He waited prudently, while they both smoked, and then he grasped it firmly.

"Well, it's a pity, Hubert," he said gaily, as though he had abandoned his attempt and could afford by now to laugh at it, "because you'd not only solve the sister problem but—look at the advertisement! 'Famous Author Weds.' 'Mr. Hubert Brett, the Novelist, who is to be married this week. Photo by Bassano.' 'Mr. Brett's beautiful young wife.' 'Mrs. Brett, wife of the celebrated author, opens a bazaar.'"

"Oh, shut up," cried Hubert quite youthfully, and made some pretence at throwing a tobacco-pouch, but did not seem displeased.

"Then," went on the remorseless friend, "she is at parties every day, and universally admired. Who is she? everybody naturally asks. Why, the wife of Hubert Brett. Have you read his new novel? If not, do."

"You must think me a conceited fool," Hubert put in, "if you imagine I swallow all that." Sometimes he suspected Boyd of sneering. Mrs. Boyd, he knew, disliked him. She had often tried a snub. She was a very brainless woman....

Kenneth Boyd dropped his manner of burlesque.

"All the same," he said, falling back into the old vein, "a wife *does* a lot in one's career, you know. She has so much more time for making friends. I always look on mine as my best canvasser! Why, man" (and now he shamelessly threw off the mask), "you simply don't know what you're missing. When I look back on my old single days, I hardly can believe that it was me or how I could have been such an almighty ass as to have wasted all those ghastly years. Perhaps, though, I shouldn't enjoy our life now so much, if I'd not had a good mouthful of the other. Good lord—the discomfort; the loneliness; the want of any one who really cares; the feeling that there's nothing *permanent*; the frantic writing round to make sure you won't have a lonely evening; the sick despair when some one fails and you sit moping by your fire or wander out among a crowd of laughing couples, damnably alone; the lack of any purpose in life; the constant cadging round for somebody to save you from a Soho restaurant. Good lord, it simply can't be true I had five years of it, and now...! Of course, Hubert, I know what you'll say. We're all different; you're not that sort; you never feel all this; you wouldn't feel as I do, if you married. But you do—you would. We're all utterly the same, deep down. You novelists forge little differences to help out your stories, but I tell you, deep down, men are all the same. We all get lonely, we all get sad and hopeless as the years go on, we want just *one* who values us more than the rest, who cares for our success, who smoothes away our failures. We can't, any one of us, get on alone. You're only shy, that's all. You funk proposing—you'd feel such a fool! But what's all that? There must be lots of jolly girls about. Just you fix on one, get married, and then come and settle down near us, out Hampstead way. Think of it! No climbing back into a grimy lodging—sorry, old man, but I mean the fogs. If you could just see Hampstead in a winter sunset! Then a nice little home, all new and clean; tea all put ready for you by your wife; the kiddies keen to see you; that's the one way, I tell you, for *all* men to come home. We're not different, a bit. We all want—*you* want—love and comradeship; we want another thing beside ourselves, in whose success we can feel proud; we want our wife, our children, and we want our home. And that's exactly what you want, my boy!"

Carried along midway, he suddenly became self-conscious and collapsed with the last sentence.

Hubert ironically clapped his hands. "Splendid, splendid! You ought to write advertisements; I'm sure the Garden City would pay a big premium. Title, 'The New Home!'"

He was much too absorbed to notice the hurt look that came over the other's face. Kenneth Boyd had been expensively educated, as a boy, in all

English ideals. He never had dared, until just now, to show his Self to any one except his wife. Now, when it was mocked at, he felt a hideous shame, a terrible resentment. And he had only wished to help his friend!

Hubert contentedly passed on to the analysis of his own state, a plea for his own attitude. "I am different, though," he said, "all the same. You can't understand. My job, for one thing, is so different. I must be left alone to do it. I *don't* ' come home,' as you so poetically put it; I'm there all the time. So would your ' kiddies' be, and they'd be a damned bore. Just when I was dying to get on with my new book, they'd be what you call 'keen to see me' and squall if I wouldn't. Oh, I can see it all. I've too much imagination, far, to need to marry; I've been through it all a thousand times, without. I can see my dear wife, as you call her, filthily jealous of my work and grudging every minute that I took for it. It's all so different for you fellows who go off to work. You've got your hours of solitude all free for business and then you come back to tea, if you're a slacker, as you've just described. But nobody ever believes that novelists do any work; it's just their hobby in spare moments! Any one may interrupt and there is no harm done. My dear wife would buzz in and out and ask me what I liked for lunch.... Oh, yes, I can see it all."

"You've no idea of it at all," said Kenneth Boyd almost passionately in his deep, sincere-sounding voice.

"And as to loneliness," Hubert went on, utterly ignoring him, "I see too many people as it is. I'm always booked. I absolutely curse them sometimes when I feel I haven't seen them for a century and they'll be getting huffy. Constant companion and all that stuff, indeed? No, thanks! Shall I tell you *my* idea of bliss?"

"This, I suppose?" the other asked, waving his pipe-stem pitilessly around the untidy room, where school football-groups mingled with Burne-Jones survivals from the Oxford age; where books usurped chairs, sofa, floor, piano-top; where no intrusive female hand was suffered, clearly, with methodic duster.

"No," answered Hubert, "though I'm fond of it. It's good enough for me as home. No, my idea of bliss is just an afternoon when I've no teas, appointments, duties, anything; when I am really free. Then I put on my very oldest suit and get out right along the river, Richmond way—Kew, Putney, anywhere—and stretch my lungs and look at the old book-shops and enjoy the river. That's when *I'm* happy, you see! I look at the river, out by Richmond Bridge, broad and festive and the sun upon it; everything all full of life; and I feel free, and that's the time I take a deep breath in—or by the sea, of course—and say, 'Thank God that I'm alive!'"

"And thank God you're alone?" his friend enquired. He looked across at him, no longer by now as at a patient, but as he might have at a curious specimen inside a labelled bottle.

Hubert was quite pleased to have this opportunity for self-analysis thrust on him. He liked to be thought peculiar but wished to be sincere. He reflected a little, then slowly blew out a funnel of smoke with energy behind it.

"Yes," he said, "and thank God I'm alone."

CHAPTER II
"WHY MEN MARRY"

Hubert shut the door after his visitor with spacerrrno deep feeling of regret. He managed to refrain from slamming it.

He was angry still.

Men are peculiar about their troubles. Woman, popularly thought to be a sieve with secrets, will crush a worry down, grapple silently and fight with it, nor ever let her very nearest know that it is there. Perhaps heroic centuries of motherhood have taught her to endure her own pain with a smile, where she can scarce bear to conceal another's folly? The man, in any case, is different. Tell him what Mrs. Tomkins stupidly said about the vicar: he will not breathe it to a living soul. Quite possibly he will not even listen to the end.... But let him have some small upset, some crisis where decision must be made, not a big choice—nothing like those he makes off-hand each day up in his city office—and you shall see him stripped of his pretence to all reserve or strength. Long time, like Homeric heroes, he sits tossing thought hither and thither. Nothing emerges from this exercise: it is a mere convention. He must think a little: people always do; but he knows well enough that not this way lies decision. He takes other steps. If he is a man of few friends, he will risk everything upon a coin's fall. "Heads I do, and tails I don't," he mutters weakly, groping in his pocket. Up spins the penny. Heads it is! "Heads I do," he murmurs once again; and adds, pathetically firm, "But all the same, I don't think I will." He has been helped to his decision.

If he has friends, he will use one of them in place of the penny. Every man, almost, has one trusted friend whose advice he does not take in all moments of perplexity.

Kenneth Boyd stood, so to speak, as Hubert's penny. He always sat and listened stolidly to his friend's trouble: then he answered "Heads" or "Tails," as it seemed best to him; went back, braced by the contrast, to his Hampstead home; and left Hubert to decide whether or no he would take the spin as final.

In this case, as he sat down, Hubert said to himself with vehemence, poking the fire fiercely, that he would not. He had asked Kenneth whether it would be mean to turn Ruth out, as she herself suggested—and he had at once embarked on a long rigmarole about dear wives, winter sunsets, kiddies, teapots, and all sorts of things....

With a last jab at the fire he dismissed the interview just over from his mind and settled down to think. He never ought to have asked that monomaniac along. He might have guessed what he would say.

Ruth was a nuisance, frankly; she jarred upon him constantly: their life was one long quarrel nowadays; but—how would solitude affect his work?

That was the big question.

To Hubert Brett his work was life, and nothing much else counted. He was a man who valued success less for its achievement than for its reward. He liked to be pointed out as one who wrote (he often was, in little country places); he enjoyed meeting men and women whose names were famous far and wide; he loved press-cuttings, revelled in his photograph when reproduced, and was almost physically upset when he received a real old-fashioned, slashing review. To anything of this sort he always replied, quoting the opinions of some other papers, and "relying on the editor's sense of justice to give his letter publicity." Papers, in fact, that liked neither his novels nor his letters, had ceased to notice the first-named, hoping to avoid the last: and he was glad of this decision. Letters from unknown readers were shown to all his friends, who also had the privilege of reading the longest reviews, left out upon his mantel-piece; though when they took them up he would always protest, "Oh, that'll bore you: it's only a few stray press-cuttings." He liked at dinner-parties to sit next women who had read his books (the dear, kind, tactful sex!), and asked him how he wrote. He had, in fact, published his first book under a pseudonym (his father, as a clergyman, naturally objecting to the real name being used), but found that no one recognised him as the author under his own different name. He therefore, on his father's death, had paid some pounds and taken the name Brett permanently as his own for ordinary use. His sister, who was like most women in being petulant as to trifles but mild about the things that matter, had submitted from being Ruth Brettesley to become mere Ruth Brett. Now, when he dined out, Hubert often found that women next him would ask if he was "the author." It never had occurred to him, of course, that they were coached by an ideal hostess.

It may be well imagined, then, that he now hesitated before taking any step that might affect his very methodical arrangements about writing. His sister, once thrown over (he told himself), would never return. She would marry or something. Women were like cats: they always did. She would not stray about uncomfortably until he wanted her again. No; she would make a home: and he, as the years went on, would find himself alone....

He had lit a pipe, and drew at it mechanically, but he was far too rapt to taste it. Kenneth Boyd's words on that one point had certainly gone home. His eyes fixed on a glowing cavern of red embers, he saw unroll before him a grisly panorama of the days to be.

He could see himself, bereft of Ruth's care, moving to a bachelor flat where they "did for" one; happy enough perhaps, at first, in solitude, and working well—happy and working until illness came. Then he saw the change. Ruth, he admitted, had been quite splendid—like her old self— when he had been ill. That was when you wanted a woman about.... Then, as Kenneth had said, he would grow older. He could see himself climbing, more and more shakily each year, the long flight to his flat; too settled far by now to move even to a lower floor. He could see the porters and people saluting—oh, so respectfully!—till he was past, and then imitating his old, broken shuffle. He could see himself turning on with fumbling hands the light he used to switch on so gaily as he dashed in thirty years ago. He could see himself all alone at night, when it was too cold for an old man to walk about and no one wanted him; sitting there with weary eyes tight closed, thinking of the friends that he would like to see, the friends all dead or—married.... And finally he could see himself climb those stairs, so full of memories, for the last time, and stagger in for the last time to that small room where he had had such jolly parties in the years gone by, and ring and have just strength to gasp out, "I must have a doctor." Yes, and that old wreck lying there, alone but for a nurse he hated, longing for sympathy, love—even Ruth's!—yes, that too would be him. And then——

For one moment the knock on his door startled him. He was like a small child who, waked suddenly, continues a bad dream. He thought that they had come with that cheap, humble coffin which he had just seen borne up the long stairs.... He very nearly cried out, "Bring it in," not realising that he was the corpse.

"Why, it's you, Ruth!" he cried in vague annoyance.

"Of course it is," she laughed. "Who else would it be, you stupid boy? Perhaps you mean, though, you don't want me?"

"Of course I always want you, old girl." This hideous geniality, he felt, was the worst part of their whole constant warfare, recalling by an empty mockery that they had once been such devoted chums; still could be, possibly, if they were only parted. "I'm not working," he added almost grudgingly, as though he wished he had got that excuse.

But Ruth, indecision personified, still hovered restlessly in mid-carpet. "Are you quite sure you're not, Hugh?" she said. "If you *are*, do say so. I've been alone all the evening till now, so it won't hurt me to go on like that till bedtime. I am used to it, you see!" and she smiled patiently.

Hubert looked at her, wondering why she possessed this curious gift of annoying him. Did she try, or was she really meaning to be kind? Her face, set and hard already, gave no hint. She smiled with her lips but her eyes did not light up. There was something tragic in her looks. She was not ugly, yet she meant absolutely nothing. She was just a passable statue, into which the artist had failed somehow to put any life. She smiled doggedly with her lips, and she clearly was not happy. She had never lived.

She went on wanly smiling reassurance at him, as one who should say, "I am not to be considered," till he schooled his voice to answer. Whatever happened, he would not have another scene on this night which seemed in some way big with a decision.

"It'll be nice to have a little chat, old girl," he said genially. "Sit down and make yourself comfy."

She moved timidly towards an armchair with the mien of a scolded, nervous child. "If you're quite, quite sure?" she quavered. "I wish I felt certain you hadn't been just thinking you would settle down, now Mr. Boyd had gone. I should be absolutely happy with my Patience."

"Boyd was in great form," Hubert answered. He could not trust himself to assure her further.

"What did he say then?" and she let herself down into the chair staidly. She was not like a woman of thirty-eight. Women of thirty-eight nowadays are young, almost unfashionably young, and Ruth was pathetically old. She had given her youth to her mother: she was prepared to lavish the rest of life upon her brother, asking in return nothing except that he would not be what she tearfully and often called unkind to her.

"Say?" answered Hubert, far more comfortably. "What didn't he say? My dear Ruth, I've had a classic homily on Marriage!"

Ruth stiffened visibly. "Marriage? Then I suppose you asked him in to give you his advice?"

"Really," said Hubert in another voice, "I imagine you can't object, now, to what I ask my pals in for?—supposing that I did."

She smoothed all that kind of thing away with a restful gesture.

"My dear boy, you know I've no objection, as you call it, to anything at all you do. You are a man. I'm only your guest. I've no right to object. But I am naturally interested. Of course, though, if you'd rather not tell me what Mr. Boyd said"—she paused, "we'll talk of something else."

"No we won't," cried Hubert, with a sudden passion. "I'm sick to death of all this constant friction."

"Friction!" and she raised her eyebrows ever so slightly. Otherwise her sad face remained expressionless, but her hands clasped each other tensely under an old-fashioned shawl.

"Yes, friction. That's the only word. You know, Ruth, I don't want to be a brute. You know what pals we were as kids, what pals we still are" (he forced the words out), "and that's why I intend to have it out. It isn't good enough. You know what a row we had over dinner. *That's* why I asked Boyd along. How do you expect a man to write when he's just had a row that's brought his soul red-hot into his throat? And you weren't very cheery company! So naturally I asked Boyd in. I often do that or go out myself or else pretend to work, because I simply can't endure your company a moment longer."

And now his sister leapt up to her feet. When she came to life it was always sudden.

"Hubert!" she cried in tearful reproach. She only called him Hubert at such moments.

He signalled her down without any ceremony.

"For goodness' sake," he said, and it was nearly stronger, "don't let's have a row." He took a moment to calm himself and then said levelly, "Look here, old girl, I want to thrash this matter out once and for all. It's no use killing love in this world, is it? It's rare enough, God knows. We've been such good pals, you and I, and now we are—like this." He pointed at her, and she fell back dully on her chair.

"We don't mean it really," she said, fumbling for her handkerchief.

Hubert spoke seriously. "We do, though. Anyhow, we should in time. It's just like other habits. It grows. It grows quickly, too. We never used to fight at all, you know."

"*I* never fight now," she protested, very near to tears. "I've always given in."

Poor, timid, self-sacrificing Ruth never could understand what her brother's tempers were about. She tried so hard not to stand up against him!

"Oh, damn!" cried Hubert, and strode madly up and down the room.

It was all very futile, quite familiar.

She looked as pained as usual. "What is it, Hugh?" she gently asked.

"Of course you've given in," he flung at her. "You always do. You're always in the right: you are so keen to be! You wouldn't make me cross for worlds! It's just your damned humility I can't endure. No man on earth could possibly endure it."

"I can't help my nature," she sobbed into her handkerchief. "I do my best to please you. I try to fall into your ways, I'm sure."

Hubert came up to her presently and touched her on the shoulder.

"I'm sorry, Ruth," he said. "It was my fault. I lost my temper. I was a cad to swear but somehow—oh, I don't know," and he sank down upon the chair again. "I suppose really it's just what Boyd has often said, brother and sister weren't ever made to live together. He says all relatives have a natural antipathy to one another and— —"

"I'm sure *I* haven't," interrupted Ruth.

This time he ignored her. "It's all so difficult," he said in a new tone, as though embarking upon an analysis. "I know you're wanting just to please me, Ruth; you are an awfully good sort; you'll make somebody a splendid wife some day; but just because you are my sister, I suppose, I get annoyed when you begin asking whether you can come in and saying you don't want to if— —"

"You'd be much more annoyed if I came in without," said Ruth, with an unwonted spirit.

Hubert rose to the attack. "You mean it's just my nature, and not you? I'd get annoyed whichever way it was? I'm just a selfish sort of cross-grained swine?"

"I didn't say so, you *know* I didn't; you're simply twisting my words round."

Grown men and women, by some odd irony, are never nearer childhood than when in a temper. Hubert realised abruptly how ridiculous it was. Once more he dropped his voice and dragged the conversation with a wrench back to the point at issue.

"I was only telling you," he said with dignity, "what Boyd said, as you asked to know. He said all this"—once more he waved his hand—"was a mistake, and that I ought to marry."

He threw it out at her like a threat at a naughty child. She would not like it if he took her at her word and really turned her out.

But even sisters can surprise a man. "Oh Hugh," she cried, forgetting all their differences, "do you mean you are really thinking——? Only, do let it be some one really nice, who'll make you as happy as you deserve to be."

He was too flustered to feel touched. "But wouldn't you mind?" he asked; and in spite of his efforts, surprise appeared in it.

"Mind?" She came across to him, sat on his chair-arm, and took his hand in hers. "How little you know me, old boy, really! Of course I shouldn't mind. You must never, never consider me at all! Do you imagine I expect you to remain a bachelor your whole life long, just to look after me? I shall find work to do or something; and anyhow, what is my life by the side of your career?"

Hubert at moments felt a brute, and this was one of them. He knew that he should thank her, kiss her, yet he could do neither. He found himself wondering in a dazed, abstract way, as often in these past years, whether she was really genuine or whether it was just a woman's bluff to make him feel his shaft had fallen short. If she was quite sincere, he felt almost aggrieved. The end of their long life together seemed to mean so little to her....

"No," he said automatically, not realising how inadequate it was; and then, "Well, old girl, I really think perhaps *now* I ought to work." He patted her hand in a perfunctory way as he released his own from it. "We've had our little chat and it's your bedtime, I am sure."

"Yes," answered Ruth, and hesitated.

"Hugh," she said presently, "aren't I to know who it is?" Her tone was more patient than aggrieved, but he read something of the other into it.

"Who what is?" he replied, although he guessed her meaning.

"Who you think of marrying. Who's suddenly put the idea into your head." She waited a few moments; then, as he said nothing, she added almost slyly, "Well, I think I know! I've not forgotten Devonshire yet, and what a lot there was in your letters about Miss—Miss—I forget her name."

"Oh, that Miss Hallam, you mean," came the icy answer.

It chilled even her exuberance. Her rare gaiety died quickly, and she looked the martyr once again.

"I see you don't mean to tell me," she said. "Very well. Of course I had no right to ask. I thought you'd like to let me know." She sighed. "I wish men weren't so terribly reserved."

"And I wish," he retorted, "that women weren't so horribly imaginative."

But she had shut the door. She always went abruptly, never said good night. He had told her, long ago, that those words broke up his evening and made him think of bed instead of work.

To-night indeed, after her going, although he had said he must do some writing, he sat quietly where he had been and gazed into the fire. He was not, however, thinking about bed. He was wondering whether all women were so crude and vulgar with their brothers. Ruth was the last person who would ever have said that about Miss Hallam to anybody else. Just because he chanced to write and say that he had met a jolly sort of girl...!

It is a stale truism about good advice, that most natures must reject it before they see their way to its acceptance. Self-pride demands that it shall be their own idea.

Just as Hubert had scoffed at his friend's idea of loneliness, which now indeed seemed such a ghastly spectre, so did he next work slowly back to the very words of his sister that had angered him the most.

For by now his mental questioning had spread across a chasm dreaded for long years and flaunted itself gaily in a narrow field.

The first step was so clear by now.

Of course he had sworn always that he would not marry, but that was true of the past only. One changed every now and then.... He was at the age when one grew lonely, when one naturally married. Sisters were a big mistake. He could not endure year after year of silly quarrels like the one just past. With a wife he would start fresh. She wouldn't irritate him like Ruth: he wouldn't see through all her motives; they need not fight for years.... Besides, he must find some one less irritating, less selfish, than Ruth.... And as to Ruth, she said herself that she was game to go. She probably preferred it. The whole thing was her own suggestion.... Yes, she was right; they certainly could not go on like this. Yet if she went—that loneliness when he got old, was ill...! Kenneth had talked a lot of drivel but he probably was right about stagnation. He found, himself, his work was getting stale.... And then the help that she——

But who?

Hubert flung himself across the chasm, refusing doggedly to see it, and found himself, flushed and excited, in the little field beyond.

Who could he marry, possibly? The question lent quite a new thrill to life. It was a big adventure, even if one never did it....

He hated clever women. He was sure of that. Hated them, at any rate, as wives. Mrs. Kenneth Boyd was one, and when he dined with them, she always waited till he had thrown out a theory, quite impromptu, possibly exaggerated rather, about something, and then said, "Really, Mr. Brett? But how unusual!" or something of the sort. No, he could not bear that. He thought that type an insult to his sex. He liked a woman to be rather silly—well, not that quite—no, but shallow. He liked her to have not too many views herself: he hated suffragettes and things, of course; but just to have the brains to understand one's own ideas. That was where the girl Ruth had mentioned was so splendid. She saw the fun of things; she even saw the fun of her name, Helena Hallam; but also she could enter into the plot of a book directly you had told it her, and be immensely interested in hearing about people you met at the Authors' Club. She was almost too ignorant, of course—knew nothing about life—but her naïve remarks amused him: so what did it matter?

That really was the sort of woman he would like to marry. Some one who would be interested in his work but know she hadn't got the brain to interfere; some one who'd look on his work-hours as sacred, because given to a thing she couldn't do to save her very life.

Ruth was annoying about that, and silly. If he read her out a chapter, she would usually say, "I think it's quite good, old boy; but I never feel you're made for fiction. I suppose essays never sell, though, and plays are quite impossible?" It was too stupid. She had said that even about *Wandering Stars*, which had sold close upon five thousand copies! Not—of course—that he valued his novels according to their sales....

The girl in Devonshire had been so different. He smiled, recalling her simplicity. She had thought him so clever to write, even before she had seen a word of it! And when he read her out a chapter, she wanted to know just how long it had taken him, asked to see how much he had corrected, and clearly looked upon the whole thing as a miracle.

Thinking of her now he had a curiously vital image of her personality. She was so fresh, so natural, so unspoilt, so splendidly a thing of life. She had never been to London. How she would love to see it; how gorgeous it would be to show! How different from taking out Ruth, who always said that the streets smelt of petrol and she had neuralgia and wished they could live in the country, but of course *he* must choose! How different altogether! How different when the lights were lit and curtains drawn! He still remembered how she sat, with one foot underneath her body, and smiled through those curiously bright eyes, as though always contentedly awaiting the next jolly thing that life could not possibly fail to bestow upon her. Ruth was so hideously gloomy and apologetic. She expected the worst but she never minded.

Yes, there was no doubt that was just the sort of sensible, unsloppy, cheerful girl that he would like to marry. She would be nice to have about the house. She wouldn't want the vote or anything. She thought so much of his work that she would never grumble, like Ruth, if he had a long bout at it. She'd take up needle-work or something. She had such a happy nature. And then at nights they'd sit and have great, jolly, sociable talks beside the fire, and he'd read out his books to her. Possibly, now and then, she would see some mistake—not in the book itself, but in a woman's dress or something: women were so good at details—and he would learn a lot, as Kenneth said, from seeing how her refreshingly simple mind regarded things. And then—she was a child—they would play games and laugh and roast chestnuts and all that sort of thing. He could imagine quite a jolly evening. The past hour seemed like a nightmare by the side of it.

He got up and mixed a whisky and soda.

Really by now he wished he had thought of all this in Devonshire! He had said to himself then, watching her, that somebody someday would be a lucky man—the girl was so herself, somehow. But it had not occurred to him that he could be the man.

Now, probably, he would never see the Hallams again. Mrs. Hallam, of course, had said they must meet soon in London, but every one always said that and it was five weeks now since his return. He had not, naturally, ever written.

Of course—there was another thrill in this idea—he could go down to Devonshire again with any false excuse trumped up; but even as this came into his head, his fatally quick fancy, over-exercised, saw him proposing to Miss Hallam, pouring out the sentimental stuff that a love-scene demanded; perhaps—who knows?—even feeling bound to kneel in the manner beloved of conventional romance!

Then, with a swift gesture, he suddenly drained his whisky and soda to its dregs, put the glass down jauntily as men do on the stage, and walked, feeling younger than for ten whole years, to his writing-desk. He gave a happy laugh as he took out some paper.

For he had got a great idea. He was going to propose to Miss Hallam on paper! He was going to write it all down and see if it looked awful rubbish.... He was enjoying himself to-night in a quite new way.

"DEAR MISS HALLAM," he began and added "My" in front. Then as he saw the meaning that might bear he laughed again. He knew it was not right just now to laugh, and marked it as an interesting fact. Then, nervous of detection, he took a new sheet and started—

"MY DEAR MISS HALLAM,

"You will be surprised to hear from me.

"The fact of the matter is—I find myself getting very bald now that I really have to use my pen for something that matters!—I have been thinking a lot of my jolly days in Devonshire, the tennis, the sea-walks, the picnics, everything with all of you, and (if I'm allowed to say it) especially with *you* yourself."

Here he leant back and read what he had written. It was not literature but he felt satisfied. He took up his pen again and wrote—

"I don't know that it's usual, but I am rather reserved and not too romantic, so that I am *writing* to ask whether you could think of being my wife. There has never been any one in my whole life of whom I have thought as I have thought of you these last five weeks. I could never tell you how I feel in words, and I see now that I can't on paper, but if you think in any way that you could grow fond of me, I am convinced that we could be immensely happy. I don't know that I have much to offer you; but if you talk to your mother about this, as no doubt you will, you must assure her that I can give you a comfortable home and that I hope, as the years go by, to make myself something of a name.

"I will say no more now. I shouldn't have dared say so much, if I had not thought that we got on rather well last month, and that if you did not welcome this letter, you would at any rate be able to forgive it.

"Yours,
"HUBERT BRETT."

It was not certainly at all like any of the love-letters that he had written in fiction or read in the police-reports; but he had not inwardly approved of either. This seemed to him quite adequate. She was the sort of girl who wouldn't care for sentiment. He honestly believed she would write back sensibly and just say "Yes."

It is to be remarked that no question remained as to posting the letter or not, so soon as it was finished. He had begun it to see how it looked: now he felt that it was something fated. He must see what happened. Without waiting even to put on a hat, he hurried out to an adjacent pillar-box and dropped the letter in with hardly more emotion than if it had been an ordinary bill.

Going up to bed, without repentance for the night's wild work, and in fact oddly calm for any one in his position, he heard a curious noise inside his sister's room.

He stopped and listened at the door.

She was obviously sobbing.

Hubert suddenly felt softened towards her. So she cared, after all! She felt the separation after these long years!

Had he sometimes wronged her? Had he been impatient? Was she really fond of him; trying to consult his wishes and not to irritate him? Was he growing selfish?...

He very nearly tapped and went in to console her. Then he reflected that she almost certainly would engineer another scene, and that always gave him a bad night.

CHAPTER III
"WHY WOMEN WED"

Helena had never thought much about marriage. There was no reason indeed why she should, for she was young and to her it still appeared, like death to a small child, as something she was sure to reach some day but need not worry with just now.

She was, in fact, nineteen, but her ideas were those of nineteen fifty years ago or of fourteen to-day. Devonshire, for one thing, has slept on in its soft air, not much disturbed by any modern turmoil; and for another, Helena's mother had ideas. These, briefly put, consisted in not letting her daughter have any.

It is, however, only human, from Eve downwards, to defy authority and search for knowledge. Helena, knowing that it was her lot to marry, naturally felt some interest in the habit. Whenever she came on allusions to it, she stocked them in her brain, all in a healthy and quite natural way, wondering in an abstract manner whether it would be thus or thus with her. She never dared to talk about it to her mother. She had once mentioned her own hypothetic marriage, only to be told that girls did not speak of such things in fun, and it would be quite time enough when the occasion rose, and had she given the canary its clean water?

Mrs. Hallam was a loving mother with stern theories. Her own childhood had been a season of repression, yet she was satisfied enough with her morals as opposed to those of many round her. She intended, therefore, to repeat the process. She had no patience—this was her favourite expression—with the licence of young girls to-day: the manner in which they read any novel, went to any play. She had no patience with this rubbish about ignorance not being innocence. Of course it was; or if it wasn't, it had very much the same result, and that was everything. Girls read these trashy novels and got a notion that grown men and women spent their whole lives falling in and out of love. They naturally tried it and began flirtation as a sort of duty. If a girl knew nothing, she did not know what to do. If she had no notion what flirtation meant, she clearly couldn't do it—especially if she saw no men till she was safely beyond her teens.

In any case, till she was twenty, Helena had no plays, novels, or man-friends. Her reading was all lives, histories, and comic papers. Her days were spent with relatives or younger friends, when she was not alone.

She grew up an oddly fine tribute to the system, thus underlining the depressing axiom which comes at length to all who study education: that those who are going to be nice will turn out nice, whatever way you train their youth, and much the same about the nasty. She was simple, healthy, buoyant, cheerful, natural; everything that Hubert thought. And who shall blame her if she was a little immature?

Hubert's letter was a real excitement in her cloistered life.

She had enjoyed her meeting with him. Men were a novelty, and to her an author was still that thing of wonder which he appeared to a suburban hostess twenty years ago. She thought him marvellously clever at first sight, and rather alarming. Later, she thought him easy to get on with and amusing. He played tennis well, liked finding crabs, and Mother did not seem to mind them talking. It was quite a jolly change. She finally thought him a dear and missed him when he left for Town.

And now—this letter!

Nothing ever could be less expected. She read it and re-read, not knowing really what she ought to do. She was just as excited and laughed as gaily as he one day before—vaguely infected, no less, with a thrill of irresponsible adventure.

Now, indeed, was the moment to collect all the vague tit-bits she had garnered as to marriage and fit them into a connected whole. She knew so little, really, of this thing that he suggested, and Mother, she knew, would not help her. The comic papers were curious about it. They looked on all men who married as fools, sure to repent; all women who didn't as ludicrously tragic. The old maid was a figure to be as much mocked and pitied as the old bachelor was to be envied.

Well, if this were so, it must be jolly hard for women to find a man who would marry! (Logic teaches that absurd premises will often lead to sensible conclusions.)

She knew vaguely that one Asked Mamma. There was a book even called that in the old locked case in the big library. She also knew, however, that she must battle this thing out herself. Her mother would say no; what nonsense! Of that she felt sure. It was for her, then, to decide.

Lock up your Danäe, stern mothers, in all the towers that man's wit may devise; yet if she is born with a strong resolve knit on her pudgy, slobbered, baby face, you cannot possibly prevail. You battle with the forces of uncounted Time.

Mrs. Hallam sat happily in her white drawing-room and read the new *Queen*, while Helena, up in her bedroom, wrestled with the letter which her mother luckily had not seen arrive.

Of course it would be a big change, she supposed? Home was a bit dull, but she had got quite used to it and one knew what to do. Having a house must be an awful business, and yet—rather thrilling! Probably Mr. Brett would make a big name; he was so immensely clever; and then they'd have a great big house, and she'd ask Mother as a guest and give her all the things she liked and said she never got in her own house! She laughed at the idea. The whole thing was tremendously amusing.

As Hubert had thought, she was laudably unsloppy. Mrs. Hallam had never let her guess that there was any sentiment in the whole world beyond maternal love. That was the heart's whole duty for a girl who was an only child that had not even seen her father.

Yes, summing it all up, she really felt the chief thing was about women having to marry or else be a joke, whereas men were a huge lark if they did. Imagine if, in all her life, she never met another man who would be fool enough! Home was very nice, of course, but horribly monotonous. She might read novels now, oh yes; the ones that Mother chose; but it was just the others that she longed to read. She felt vaguely (for self-development is among the instincts natural to Man), that there was something being *kept* from her. She had not been meant, ever, to remain so ignorant. She felt that Mr. Brett would not wish to keep her back in the way Mother had. Besides, if she remained at home, some day her mother would die, and she be left— that dreaded thing—an old maid, all alone, for every one to mock. Nobody would want her then! Wouldn't it be awful to feel you had thrown away a chance that lots of women, she had gathered, never got? Fancy being Helena Hallam, that absurd name, all your life! H. H., one of her uncles had called her stupidly, and she had said then that it sounded like poor Miss Jowett in the village, whom everyone called "old J. J.," because her name was Jane. Oh yes, she would end at last as old H. H.—poor old H. H.—pottering about in her prim little garden with an antiquated, rat-like dog dragging itself crookedly along behind her. All the village poor would be so sorry when she died.

She shuddered at the thought. She always wanted to put poor J. J.'s old dog, the one with the pink satin bow, out of its misery. It would be kind, she knew. She could with the air-gun, but Mother had seemed really shocked.

She suddenly decided at this point that her thoughts had become depressing and not really helpful towards a decision. Without giving herself time to feel alarmed, she rose abruptly and went to the drawing-room.

She knew instinctively she must be firm.

This was the first thing ever that had really mattered, mattered to *her* as a separate person with a life to live, and she believed she knew already what she ought to do. She would listen, of course, to Mother's views—she owed that from a real love and gratitude—but she would not be bullied any longer.

She entered the room feeling herself in some way on a different footing. The latent, undeveloped thing that would be Helena had surged towards birth at a mere spark from the outer world.

"Mother," she began, quite simply, "I've had a letter from Mr. Brett. He has asked me to marry him and I think I rather shall."

Mrs. Hallam dropped her *Queen*. She did not often find herself surprised.

"You've what, dear?" she asked blankly. Then not waiting for any reply, "What do you know about marriage, my dear child? What do you know about Mr. Brett?"

"I don't want to be an old maid," answered Helena, playing her best card at once.

Mrs. Hallam met it with a scornful laugh. "Old maid!" she cried. "That is a preposterous idea you've got out of your comic papers."

"They're all I've ever read, histories and them," Helena said mildly; raising who shall say how many bitter doubts in the breast of a theorist.

"You're nothing but a child, my darling girl," the mother said more gently; "and even if you weren't, there's no disgrace in being what you call an old maid. Some of the world's best women have been that. You've got to think of far more serious matters than that before you can possibly decide on such a step as marriage;" and searching frantically for objections which she felt sure must exist, she fell back on her first thought. "What do you know about Mr. Brett?"

"I liked him better than any of the men I've met."

"You've not met *any* yet," snapped Mrs. Hallam; she had no patience with this nonsensical idea. Then, as her girl was silent, she realised that here too she had flung out a taunt mainly against her own theories.

Mrs. Hallam loved Helena with real devotion, and it was a torture now to feel that possibly her care had all been a mistake; had all been shipwrecked by the unexpected action of an extraordinary man. She knew for a fact— she had taken care—that she and he had not indulged in any sentimental rubbish. Mr. Brett had seemed to hate all that, and she had for this very reason asked him round so often. Helena and he had been like boy and girl, brother and sister, playing games or finding their dear jelly-fish and crabs together, whilst he had talked to her in just the way to broaden her views out a bit yet not stretch them too far. And now— —!

It really was provoking. The silly girl—all girls were silly—would of course exalt him into the fine figure of her first love, the real man for her, the man that she was not allowed to marry....

Mrs. Hallam, always frail and white, seemed to shrink visibly beneath this trouble. She held out a thin hand to the puzzled Helena, and drew her down beside her on the sofa.

"Look here, dear," she said gently; "I want to talk seriously to you. Life isn't so easy as you think. I've kept you here, safe from all worries and responsibilities and guarded you so that everything has seemed quite simple; but there *are* worries and responsibilities. You've got to live your life now, you see, Helena, and you will have to learn the habit of making quick choices whether you go this way or that. Life is full of cross-roads, you will find, and not all of them lead right. You can't marry the first man you meet just because he asks you to. Later on you might meet some one who, you would then see, is the man you ought to have married.... I don't want to put such terrible ideas into your head, dear child; I've never spoken to you of them, but such things have occurred and may occur again."

Helena was really quite excited. This was the first, almost, she had ever heard of life and it seemed utterly tremendous. She was tired of having choices made for her. She felt a call to the cross-roads. She waited silently for more.

"You see, dear," went on Mrs. Hallam, pressing her child to her as though she could not at all afford to let her go and be left all alone, "you're young, very young, and though I've never told you, very beautiful. You need not fear about being an old maid!" whereat, half laughing and half crying, she kissed Helena, too dazed almost to respond. "That will be possibly life's most important choice. Don't make it, darling child, until you're fit for it. Stay with me," and there was a pathetic appeal in her words, "stay with me till I've taught you how to be reliant. You are a child still; I've kept you young; I hope I have been right; you're not fit to go out and grapple with the world. Stay with me, Helena; tell Mr. Brett that he must wait, and stay here, in your home, until I've made you strong enough to take your part in life."

"Stay here?" Helena repeated automatically.

For one brief moment the barred gates had swung open and she had gained a glimpse at life, its dangers and responsibilities perhaps, but all its splendid thrill and glorious chance. The few cold words from her prim mother had conjured up a rich glowing picture to this girl, who for years had chafed at the narrow round, longing for something—she knew not what, but something broader, something where she could be much more herself—longing, she knew now, for freedom and for life.

Mrs. Hallam looked at her with pain in her eyes.

"Aren't you happy, haven't you been happy here?" she asked.

"Why of course I have, you dearest of dear old mums," cried Helena, and pressed her lips against her mother's cheek; "but——," and she hesitated.

"But——?" asked her mother, smiling sadly. How ridiculous, how almost tragic, it all was! She threw back her mind to her own first romance and wondered where the man was now. "But——? Tell me, dear. I shall quite understand and I am sure you need not feel afraid of me!"

Helena thought deeply. Words were so difficult.

"But——," she said once again; and then, suddenly inspired, she started rapidly; "Well, it is what you said just now. I—I *must* live my own life. I want—I want to grow. I've not grown since I was fifteen. I felt so silly, like a child, when I was talking to—to Mr. Brett, and I am twenty now." She said this most imposingly.

"And so," said Mrs. Hallam, trying not to smile, "you want to marry Mr. Brett because he made you feel so silly when you talked to him?"

Helena flushed, still sensitive to ridicule. "I want to marry Mr. Brett," she said with dignity, "because he is clever, and being a fool, I admire cleverness more than anything in the whole world, and I believe *he'd* let me expand."

"Do you mean I have kept you back?" asked her mother, in low, earnest tones. She had accused herself.

"No, you've been splendid." Helena patted her hand. "No girl ever had such a good mother.... And now you are going to be good about this too, and not be troublesome and try to keep me here!" She jumped up and stood facing her, excitement and expectancy.

Mrs. Hallam was suddenly conscious of her weakness.

It had been so easy to be strong when she was dealing with a child— and she had kept Helena a child. Now, in this moment, she realised that she was dealing with a woman, a woman of a stronger will. Something, Mr. Brett perhaps, had altered Helena. Even her way of talking had changed in an instant.

"Expand" and "troublesome"——! She looked up and saw before her no longer an obedient child, but a girl almost bursting with the desire to live at nearly any cost.

Mrs. Hallam was naturally alarmed. She knew that any contest of the wills was useless. She fell back upon pathos.

"Helena dear," she said weakly, "you're twenty now. I don't want to dictate to you, to treat you as a child. You have the right, as you say, to live your own life. But do you think it right," and now her voice grew very feeble, very plaintive, "after I've done all I have for you, not to think of me at all?"

"What do you mean?" asked Helena with quite an emphasis upon the second word. She felt a dim mistrust of this new tone. She had been kindlier to opposition, for indeed at the moment she almost longed to fight.

Mrs. Hallam, anxious to explain, to justify once and for all, began again at the beginning.

"All these years, dear child, though you did not, could not of course guess it, I've been moulding you according to a theory of my own; not a new theory but what is far better, one that has stood the test of centuries. I wanted to form your character, your will, before you were brought face to face with life. That process is not quite complete yet, although you seem to think it is." She spoke the last words rather bitterly, then with a sudden change to gentleness, went on, "But even if it had been, do you think that when I've given up the best years of my life to you, it is fair for you to dash away, leaving me alone, and not to give me the reward of spending a few pleasant years with the dear child I have helped to form?"

She smiled lovingly, but Helena looked coldly back at her. It was the other's point of view, to her, which was not fair.

"I don't see that," she answered almost fiercely, surprised at her own words, oddly unlike herself of one hour ago and many years before. "*That's* not living your own life a bit. *You* didn't give those best years of your life to your mother. I shall often see you, and I expect you did yours. You gave the best years of your life to your daughter, you say, and I want to give my best years to mine."

Mrs. Hallam loathed excitement, thinking it bad form; but now she raised her voice. "My dear!" she cried. "Where did you get these most extraordinary notions? Was it from this Mr. Brett?"

"You said you liked all his ideas so much," laughed Helena, "and yet you're shocked because I want to marry him!"

"There is a difference, dear," retorted Mrs. Hallam, her calmness regained, "between liking a man's ideas and caring for him as a son-in-law."

Helena, however, in her new mood wanted something more direct than generalities. "What have you got against him then?" she flashed.

Mrs. Hallam spread her thin hands soothingly. "Nothing, dear, absolutely nothing. Do not let us have a scene. I thought him a charming man; possibly rather self-centred, but clever, cultured, and with, I am sure, good motives. I feel certain he will do extremely well. If you had wished to marry him in five years—but at twenty— —!" She spoke as though it were fourteen.

"Well," remarked Helena slowly, as though reviewing the whole situation from impartial ground, "I suppose the wedding won't be to-morrow. Don't you usually wait a bit?"

Her mother noticed that there was no hypothesis—no "wouldn't be"—about it. She saw no good in a conflict. The girl was twenty, the man probably twelve or more years older; there was nothing, she almost regretfully admitted, to be said against him; they had seemed good chums. Most mothers would have been delighted, for he was making himself a name as a novelist. Yet she was not, for he had come with this preposterously worded letter to wreck all her plans. She had thought him so safe, from the mere fact that he had no romance or sentiment about him. He was so safe, yes, for Helena; a real platonic friendship; opening her eyes a little to the bigger world outside, but altogether to be trusted not to put ridiculous ideas into her head. He was the first man with whom she had ever trusted Helena at all alone, and now— —!

"Mother," laughed Helena, suddenly clasping her fondly round the neck, "I can see from your cross face you *do* mean to be troublesome! Now just be good instead and say that we may be at any rate engaged? It will be such fun, and we can see then how we feel about it."

Mrs. Hallam by now knew with all certainty that she was weak. She felt a vague sense of relief that Helena had asked permission; at one moment she had not expected that.... If she refused it, what would be the end? Possibly elopement, suicide, or some other of those awful means that modern girls employed so freely.... Whereas if she said yes, she still retained her grip as mother and might use what authority she had to disillusion slowly this girl, who looked on her engagement as mere fun.

"Very well, my own dear daughter," she said and suddenly found herself crying.

To Helena also things had turned out otherwise than she expected. She had not ever thought that she would get her mother's leave. For one moment it was almost a shock! She felt suddenly thrust out beyond recall upon a journey all mysterious to her. She was not sure, now, that she ever meant to do more than assert her right to do just as she wanted.

Did she want to marry Hubert Brett? She was not really sure.

She wanted certainly to get away from Home....

Five more years of this—that was what her mother hinted at—five more years of being ignorant, of seeing no one, knowing nothing about anything that mattered, being just your mother's daughter—five more wasted years!...

So that, after having dried her mother's tears and told her, very truly, how much she had always and would always love her, she hurried upstairs to her writing-desk with quite a new sensation of life being a most vital and palpitating thing. Her days had been all terribly alike: this was so different and thrilling!

The only thing was—how did one begin?

She wished she had asked Mother. She couldn't very well go down and ask her now. Besides, she might just change her mind.

"Mr." looked so stiff like that; yet she did not like, quite, to call him Hubert yet.

She gave a little laugh of excitement. What fun it all was! She wondered if other people felt like this, when they were getting married. They probably knew all about it?

Oh yes, of course; she'd go by his letter....

But no; because when *he* wrote they were not engaged!

So finally she thought it best to leave a blank and start straight off—

"I really don't know at all what I ought to say. I am no good at letters and this is very difficult, but I too enjoyed all our walks and things, and if you really want to marry me I don't see why we shouldn't be engaged. I liked you very much down here and hope I shall make you happy. Mother doesn't seem very keen about it, I think she thinks I am too young though I am twenty, but she has given her consent and will, I am sure, come round to it, so don't worry.

"I'm afraid you'll think this letter very stupid, but you know how ashamed I always was of my ignorance. I seem to know nothing! It is very nice indeed of any one like you to care for me.

"Yours,

"HELENA HALLAM.

"P.S.—You won't be able to tease me any more about my name, afterwards!"

Perhaps to any real anthologist or expert of love-letters this would seem but little better than the attempt it answered; yet if success must be judged by results, it cannot have been much amiss, since for the first time in his life Hubert Brett was melted to a display of ridiculous emotion. "Dear little girl!" he murmured aloud and kissed the last words before her signature.

As for Helena, having run out to the village and posted the letter unread by her mother—a cause of yet further misgiving to the theorist—she began to wonder ever so little whether she had done quite wisely.

From somewhere (who can say whence, since some things are inborn in Man?) she had got the notion, possibly ridiculous, that courting and proposals were quite different from this. Even in the Lives and comic papers men knelt and that sort of thing. She felt she had been cheated rather of Romance.

As things were, with her so ignorant and Mother like that, it was all a little of a worry.

But it was also a way out....

CHAPTER IV
HYMEN

If Hubert had known how difficult a job it was to get married, he would never have attempted it. Or so at least he told himself. All Boyd's advice, all his own misgivings about lonely age, all Ruth's scenes, would not have driven him to so much real hard work that had no definite connection with his mapped and beloved life-career.

He always had imagined that the thing took half an hour, and even then was managed by some luckless friend you roped in as best man. And here he was, worried all day about presents, relatives, guests, leases, settlements, and heaven itself even probably could not say what else, till he despaired about his autumn work.

Ruth, in particular, drove him almost frantic.

He was absolutely certain she loathed his marrying, and yet to judge from the outside, nothing in the whole world could have pleased her more than making the arrangements. She would talk for forty minutes about buying six new pairs of socks. Her air of Willing Service maddened him. When she had nothing else to do, she would divide her time between telling him that he was a cold lover and assuring him that there was no need whatsoever to worry about her. *She* would be all right. He mustn't think of *her*....

"I don't," he would hurl back at length, firmly convinced of her hypocrisy (he was a great believer in his intuitions), at which point she usually cried. Then he would go out and shake the pictures crooked by slamming the door. At their next meeting, all forgiveness, Ruth would take up again the subject of those socks.

Finally he abandoned all idea of finishing his novel. This would be the first blank autumn since he started writing. He felt cross with Fate.

In all this, romanticists will no doubt be gratified to hear, Helena was the sole consolation.

He was pleased with her—and he was pleased with his own cleverness in having lit upon her. If marriage was essential to him, he felt sure she was just the very girl to be a wife who wouldn't get upon his nerves. The more he saw of her, the more he liked her; and that, too, was encouraging. She had, of course, come up to London with her mother, no less busy than himself, and her delight with the great shapeless place—its crowds, its fogs, its lights—was beautiful to see. She never wanted to be taken to theatres or show-places; the spectacle of London being London was enough for her, as it should be, indeed, for any one. She loved the ceaseless motion, the sense of something getting done; the whole feeling of energy massed in a little space seemed to inspire this girl used only to the sleepy, uneventful fields.

"Well, and how do you like it? How does it strike you?" he asked, as from an omnibus he showed her, for the first time, that thrilling crowd which passes, ant-like, this way and that, seemingly purposeless yet always full of purpose, past the Bank of England. He loved to hear her quaint, unformed ideas.

Helena thought for a moment. "It makes me feel so *useless*," she replied.

She was a delightful child, Hubert told himself—unspoilt, original, and modest. When he forgot about his ruined novel, he certainly was happy. His unhid admiration helped a little to melt Mrs. Hallam, who was still looking pathetically for the absolute objection which she felt sure she ought at last to find. And all this while the day was coming near.

Mrs. Hallam had rather naturally planned that the wedding should take place in Devonshire; but the bridegroom had been so hideously shocked, and Helena thought a London wedding so much better "fun," that Mrs. Hallam, already feeling nobody, had given in to them with a weak smile. She did not mind where it took place, so long as they were happy and it was really for the best. Besides, she had a brother who lived in a big house in Langham Place. He always had been very mean, and was a bachelor, and it was time altogether that he did something for the family....

On the last night, however, before the wedding-day, she tuned herself at bedtime to a final effort. She was sad and depressed: they had talked long downstairs; her own instinct would have been to cry or go to sleep; but she decided that, for her own later peace of mind if for no higher motive, she must do something far less pleasant. So along she went to the second-best spare-room in the mean brother's house.

"Helena dear," she said, to meet her daughter's startled look, "I've come along, although we've had our talk downstairs, because I feel I can't sleep till I have asked you a question."

Helena was not greatly reassured. She had not really understood a lot of what her mother had sobbed out to her downstairs, and now when she had thought it all over and had been feeling very sorry for the poor lonely dear, there was to be another question!

"Why, what?" she asked, trying to put away unseen her going-away hat, which she had been trying on. She was afraid her mother might think it unfeeling.

"A very important question," answered Mrs. Hallam, dropping frailly on the sofa. "And I'm afraid you may think it an extraordinary one. Do you really love Hubert? Do you really want to marry him?"

Helena let go of the hat, which fell very gently on the floor beside the dressing-table; then she went across and put her arms around her mother.

"Why, you curious old dear," she said. "What on earth makes you ask that? I *do* call it extraordinary!" And she laughed.

But her mother was serious. "Don't think it would be wrong or wicked to say no if you do not. It would be very wicked not to...." She paused, and as Helena said nothing, she went on; "You see, darling child, I feel responsible. You are so young, and Mr. Brett being almost the first man you ever spoke to, except just at At Homes and so on— — It's not too late, my dear girl, although perhaps I should have spoken sooner if I could have brought myself to it. Girls often see more clearly at the last. We can easily announce that the wedding is postponed, and then you could come down home for a few months and see—if you're not sure— —"

She spoke almost keenly by now, questioning with a hope quite pathetic. The world for her held nothing but her daughter.

In Helena, however, the words raised a depressing vision.

Home—Devonshire—the lanes and muddy fields—the vicar—the farmyard—the illustrated papers—the picked novels—the dull people—her dear, good mother's absurd care of her.... And then, flashing and dazzling by its contrast, London—its crowds and mystery—its freedom—Hubert, so brilliant and kind—those jolly times with him beside the sea or on the 'bus-tops—the talks on Art and Life and all the things she couldn't understand but longed to—the liberty to cease being a fool and ignorant—the open gate to real existence....

"I *am* sure," she answered, with a passion that surprised herself. "Quite sure." She was not sure about love, but she wished to marry....

Hubert, in fact, wanted to escape his fond sister and a lone old age; Helena desired to get away from a loving home and her own ignorance. It is quite possible to fall in love with even negative abstractions.

At any rate they were very fond of one another, and practised wedding-goers were able to make their usual remark: "How utterly devoted they seem! It is so nice to see them look at one another!"

Everybody said too, of course, that Helena had never looked so pretty. She had been arranging presents until one o'clock and not left time to get her hair in order, besides having been dog-tired for a week, and the wedding-veil is seldom becoming, but all the guests seemed pleased. Certainly, with bright eyes sparkling ever so gaily behind the old veil of Argentan lace, and little wisps of hair exuding everywhere, Helena, if not at her best, looked natural and young.

Hubert, on the other hand, looked old for his age and self-conscious as only a man can look at his own wedding, but yet unusually handsome. He had not recovered from the dismal farce of a bachelor dinner, where nobody had liked the champagne, the idea of speeches had fizzled out, and every one had gone home before ten o'clock. He was pale and nervous. Yet Helena's relatives decided quite honestly, and in fact unexpectedly, that he was a good-looking man, and even Helena was quite surprised. His new Sunday coat revealed a slim, tall figure generally hidden by old, well-loved tweeds, for he was not a London-dresser. A stiff collar made the greatest change in him, and (had he but guessed!) so soon she decided he must always wear one. His very agony improved his looks. Of the dark, clear-cut type, he was spoilt usually by a too erratic mouth, which rambled on his face and lent a look of weakness to the stern contour. To-day his lips were pressed and firm. He felt a fool and told himself that the whole business was astounding rubbish. If only she had liked it, he would have been married at a registrar's—or down in Devonshire!... He went about with an air of doom among the revellers, and all of them said once again, if with more truth than about Helena, that they had never seen him look so well.

"Only shows," whispered Mrs. Boyd, who did not love him or any author over-much, "that those artistic people could easily look gentlemen. It's nothing but a pose."

None the less, it was a genuine enough relief to Hubert when the time came at which he was able to go upstairs and shed his fair raiment. True, they were not his old tweeds that he was allowed to don, nor was the collar soft; but still he felt more himself as he hastily descended one flight and then waited ten minutes, with all of a new husband's still untamed impatience, for his wife to be ready.

At last, when he was within four minutes of being able to feel justified in shouting out that they would miss their train, Helena appeared: full of amused excitement, still thinking it all the greatest of great fun and very sweet in a quite married-looking velvet gown, with the most colossal muff that matched a very cloud of furs, and over all of it a plume that waved above her never steady hat until it looked like a pillar of thin smoke.

Hubert, all impatience, quite forgot to say that she looked charming. It was really lucky she had not been taught yet to expect it.

"Come along," he said instead. "We're getting a bit late. I rather dread this part!"

"Oh, I don't know," she laughed. She had loved all of it.

They went down to the lower flight, where all the guests were pitilessly ranged on each side of the broad Georgian stairs.

Of course there was the funny man, who will happen even in the best-born families. Perhaps he has some use at such a time as this. Ruth and Mrs. Hallam, both united in feeling tearful yet mutually hostile, found amusement in his constant parrot-cry of "Here they are!" or when he felt specially inspired, even "Here they aren't!" It was a relief to have any excuse at all to laugh.

And there at length they were, smiling gaily, shaking countless hands, quailing under genial pats, avoiding silver horseshoes and gold slippers. (Rice and confetti were vetoed by the mean brother.) And so into the car, with Ruth and Mrs. Hallam smiling crookedly through tears, until the funny man, dutifully fumbling with string and an old slipper, was lost in a vast cloud of steam or something white let out by the fresh-started engine, which sent the couple off amid a bellow of good-omened laughter, and every one surged in with relief to say good-bye and to agree they should have gone away much earlier. It had been hideously long, but weddings always were.

Helena, as a corner blotted out the house, came back into the car with a gay laugh.

"Got your camera, my dear?" asked Hubert. It is odd how soon a man acquires the air of a proprietor.

"I *wish* I'd thought of taking them as we went off," said Helena. "They looked so funny."

He made no reply. He seemed to be thinking. She wondered what about. Then, as he sat silent, she began to be afraid to interrupt his thoughts. Besides, she did not know quite what to say. It was so curious! She realised, with rather a shock, how little really she knew about this man, and here she was going away alone with him for life!... But probably brides always felt like that? It was a biggish thing to do, anyhow, getting married. She expected it would feel a bit funny with any one. Probably the man made very little difference....

And presently he spoke—if it is speaking to say, "Ah!"

They were at Charing Cross.

They had agreed to take old baggage and look a very long-established couple, but somehow porters and people were nudging each other with sympathetic joy long before they reached the first-class carriage with its wickedly big label marked "engaged."

Helena, embarrassed if amused, sat on the far side. Hubert leaned out of the window and bought all the evening papers. He knew that there had been reporters.

"May as well see what they put," he said, almost as though in apology. She could not understand his tones, but Mother had told her last night that men were funny things with curious ideas.

He took up one after another and flipped through them all.

"Solemnised—Langham Place—écru lace," he read from the first; and then more hurriedly, "Reception—residence—numerous and costly—happy couple—Riviera."

Judging from his extracts, Helena thought, they were all very much alike. She wondered if one man had written the whole lot, and if so, what all the rest of the reporters did.

Her husband's face grew blacker as he reached the last. He threw it down with a contemptuous laugh.

"Why, what is it?" she asked. "Don't you like them?" She still felt oddly shy about using his name. "Are you disappointed?"

"One doesn't expect much from journalists," he said. "One's never disappointed."

But he was.

One account said that he was "a" novelist, but that was all: no adjective before it, not even "well-known." The others didn't mention that he *was* an author.

They might have been just ordinary people.

PART II
HUBERT BRETT'S WIFE

CHAPTER V
ROUTINE

It was something of a career, Helena soon learnt, to be the wife of Hubert Brett.

Gradually, however, she got a grip of the rough lines of her whole duty. At first it had been difficult, for she was not methodical by nature; but now it all seemed natural, the ordinary thing. When you got into it, the day ran smoothly. She never even had to think by now. She had the housemaid's mind.

Everything in the little garden suburb home—for Hubert, capitulating to Kenneth Boyd all along the whole line, had settled out at Hampstead—every smallest detail was ordered to one end: the Work.

This, he reminded her so soon as they returned to England, was not just his pride or hobby: it was their existence. She had her three hundred pounds a year, which he wished her to keep, whilst his fixed income was a trifle less—his father had been that fatal sort of mongrel, half a cleric, half a City man—and for the rest they must depend upon his writing. How important then, but how essential, that he should be left free to do his very best.

"You're my little housekeeper," he told her playfully the first evening, always loving to treat her as a child. "You'll get new cooks about every other day and try new dishes out of shilling books with them, and I shall say: 'My dear, this isn't edible'—like that—and then you'll cry——"

"Oh no, I shan't!" she laughed back, for they got on extremely well in an unsentimental way. It was almost as though Hubert had merely exchanged his sister for a younger one.

"Well, I like to think you will," he answered. "I shall be hurt if you don't mind in the least when I'm cross.... But what I was going to say is: whatever domestic tragedies there are—and kitchens are the last home in England of poor Tragedy—don't bring them round to me. I don't mind *what* I eat, I'm very tame that way really; but I don't want to know who cooked the chop or where the large woman who cooked the last one is. Those details don't inspire an author, even with a realistic novel!" The which she thought great fun. She loved to hear him talk.

None the less, it was not easy just at first. There was a hideous lot to remember for any one not good at lessons. The kitchen with its rows of plates, and all the currants and things you served out from tins—this was quite splendid. The hours and what you mustn't do were the real worries.

Hubert Brett, in the old days of city life, had never breakfasted till half-past nine. "They sleep in the city, and more is the pity, but you on the hills, awake!" exhorts the Harrow song. But Hubert did not see it in that light at all. Nine-thirty had been his hour down in London; nine-thirty seemed quite good enough up on the Hampstead hills. So nine-thirty it was—when it was not nine-forty-five.

This was the one fixed meal of the day.... Now work put in its claim.

At breakfast, he told people, was the only time that he could skim the daily; he was so intensely busy; and certainly he propped the *Telegraph* before him on the table every morning (this shocked Helena at first, for she had not seen any farces and had no notion it was ever done); but somehow or other he appeared never to have quite finished just the paragraph that he was reading when the meal concluded. There was an armchair temptingly near alike to table, fire, and cigarettes.

Helena's first important duty was to steer him tactfully from this chair to the harder one whereon he sat to write. She must not jar him, must not hurry him, or he lost every one of his ideas, and it was all her fault at lunch.... But, on the other hand, she must not let him sit there, gazing at a thrice-read page—"thinking out my day's work," he called it—till too late. This she certainly did not desire to do, for Lily never was allowed to come and clear the meal away till he had gone into his study (that upset him, too), so that delay bred chaos in the household.

When once, however, he was safely at his writing-table, all was quiet, must be, until lunch-time. These were his best hours for work. The small house brooded under a funereal silence.

Lunch was a movable affair.

Hubert could not endure clocks in his working-room. Their sound, which he declared was just not regular, got on his nerves, and he found himself on days when his inspiration would not flow, gazing at the dial with growing despair, like a bad sleeper who begins to count the hours which strike at ever lessening intervals, until he knows at last that now he will not sleep at all.

The writer's estimate of time varied largely with the amount of his success. When he was writing well, the hours would speed away and he would then emerge at half-past two or even—once—at three, full of a joy so intense as to ignore, or even to melt, the iciness of Helena and Lily. At other times, when his pen dragged itself along the paper sleepily or idly drew vague circles on the blotting-pad, he would get tired and hungry. On these days lunch was punctual at one o'clock.

After lunch, which was a meal solid almost to the limits of bad art, he would subside on the tempting armchair again and Helena be asked to bring him the weekly reviews. Not only the literary pages were digested; Hubert read the music, art, even the drama columns—everything except the science meetings in the *Athenæum*. This took, roughly, half-an-hour each day and the lonely time so occupied, he told Helena when he explained his ways to her, was devoted to "keeping in touch with the modern movements." There is no one English word for the Italian *siesta*.

Then came the part of the day to which Helena looked forward; the afternoon, when they took ever such long tramps with Spook, the small white Aberdeen, across the wide free heath, and so home to tea beside a comfortable fire. Helena could almost hate his work when at the stroke of five he would get up, more stern by now than in the sleepy morn, and leave her with the statutory kiss. And when it rained, so that this jolliest part of the day was lost and he said in a masculine way that it would be a chance to do some letters (instead of having fun indoors!), she would sit by the drenched windows and look out through the jerky raindrops with all the pathetic grievance against Fate of children in a seaside lodging on wet holidays.

This was a shorter bout of work and dinner was generally not later than half-past seven, though there were times of course when it had to be later. This led to Hubert's prophecy about the change of cooks not being too far from inspired.

After dinner was the other jolly time, if Hubert had worked well. If things had gone badly, he would mope and say that he was going to grow cabbages instead and silly things like that, which worried her because she knew he never would; but if a good sheaf of written paper was in his hand, he would read it to her, while she sat against his legs upon the hearthrug, and when she had said how good it was, they talked of other things—he talked so well—and it was all as comfy as could be in their own little home, and, oh, so different from Devonshire!

Sometimes she felt guilty about her poor mother, down there all alone among those stodgy people; but she wrote to her every Sunday, and sometimes on other days if Hubert was silent and gloomy (without of course letting her know why she wrote).

His moods puzzled her a good deal in those first days, but she supposed all really clever men were a bit odd or they would not be clever. Certainly it was curious that Hubert, who was so strong and splendid in most ways, was so awfully easily pleased or upset by anything about his books. Any success made him as cheery as could be and they would go to Kew or somewhere and he'd say; "Blow the evening work!" although she always said she was not sure they ought. Once, a few months after the wedding, a reader wrote to him from Surbiton and thanked him for a book of his he had just read, because he thought it beautiful and full of inspiriting ideas. Of course she had been immensely pleased, but Hubert had been more. He had shown it to every one who called for three weeks, and kept on wondering what sort of person could have written it, and left it about on tables, and she was sure the servants read it, and he told Mr. Alison about it twice, until she really began to wonder whether people wouldn't laugh at him, but didn't say so because he was so sensitive.

It was always the same, about a good review or anything. Sometimes, after one, he would ask in a thoughtful, puzzled way; "Why don't we ever go to a theatre, dear?" but by the next night something had probably upset him or he forgot, and she never reminded him because he *did* work hard — and, as he said, for *her* — and she was really very happy in their little home, so long as he was not at work.

And then, he was so easily upset.

A bad review had just the opposite effect. He got so violent about the critics, saying they were men who had failed to create, and any ass could say that elephants were rotten things but it took God to make one, and other awful things like that; or else he'd begin thinking who of his pals read the paper where the criticism was and sometimes even — if she couldn't stop him — write and tell them why the critic was so down on him, which she was half afraid they must think very silly; unless, perhaps, they were clever too, so understood.

Once, too, at the end of the first year, he quite frightened her.

Among their wedding presents, duly numerous and costly — perhaps extreme in both respects for a suburban home — the one that Helena prized and used most was an enamelled watch. It was the size, roughly, of a shilling: deep translucent blue, decked with tiny pearls, and hung from an appropriate brooch by a thin golden chain. Too thin possibly, for on arrival home one morning from what she called her marketing, the little gewgaw, valued for ornament and use alike, was gone. A few links of the chain hung desolately from a brooch that, robbed of its purpose, now looked almost vulgar.

Without thinking, without reflecting that no one was allowed to interrupt him before lunch-time, she found her thoughts turning restfully, in quite a wifely way, to Hubert. She knocked at his door.

There was no answer but she had not waited for one. She burst in.

The room was full of industry. The very air seemed heavy with a wished-for silence. A clock would have been overpowering.

Hubert swung slowly round, with an expression on his face that made it clear he was attempting not to lose touch with some great idea. He kept a finger on the sheet before him.

Helena was rather alarmed. She had not seen his study in its present state, and as she stood there at the door a moment, her eyes took in the litter of loose paper; all the open books on table, chairs, and floor; the derelict type-writer, long abandoned as fatal to all inspiration; the velvet coat; and most of all, the worried look. Her plaint shrank instantly to an excuse.

"Oh Hugh," she said (she never could quite manage "Hubert"), "I *am* so sorry, but what do you think?"

"I can't imagine," he said in a cold voice so unlike his own. "What? Is your mother dead?"

Even Helena, so bad at scenting irony, could guess that he did not mean that.

"Of course she isn't," she replied; "but I've lost the lovely little watch she gave me, and I did love it so." She tried not to let too much sorrow come into her voice. He always looked upon her as a baby, anyhow.

Surely he was sorry? He said nothing. He looked at her so oddly that she grew alarmed.

"Isn't it awful?" she added uneasily.

Hubert rose slowly to his feet. "Really, Helena," he said, "you don't mean you've broken my whole morning's work just to tell me you've lost some silly trinket? You might have waited until lunch-time. Now, my whole chapter—well, it simply means I've got to start it all again."

He took up a sheet of paper, tore it dramatically through, and let the two halves fall upon the carpet. Helena, full of an astounded guilt, looked down to see how much of his work her thoughtlessness had wasted. But all the writing must have been upon the under side....

"Oh, Hugh dear," she said, longing to touch him yet not daring quite; he looked so cross and tall. "I *am* sorry. It was stupid of me. But I thought you'd be sorry and could—could do something."

She ended lamely and he was not touched by her faith in him.

"Of course," he said bitterly, "I shall at once scour the heath, like a police dog, on my hands and knees. I shall watch the termini. I shall telephone——"

"Oh, I *am* sorry," she broke in, "awfully. I never thought all that of course. I simply felt it was so terrible and you might help, because you always know about things, somehow."

That touched him at last. He melted suddenly.

"Well," he said quite cheerily, "it's done now, so bother the old work. We'll see if we can't find the thing and save a reward. That's another way of making money, eh?"

So after cross-examination as to routes and so on, out they went, and he it was who found the watch, exactly where—she now remembered—she had felt hot and pulled hard at the stiff clip of her chinchilla stole.

"Tally-ho!" he shouted gaily, holding it aloft and waving it; then as she ran delightedly across from her own line of search, "so I've not wasted my day's work in vain!"

She felt that more apologies must take the place of thanks. She also wished that she had never spoilt his work but paid five pounds reward instead. And she resolved that nothing short of thieves or fire would take her into his room before lunch again.

Bad news, hereafter, she obediently kept till dinner. His day's work was over, and he had recovered by next morning's bout.

Other things, too, she learnt. When possible, she would suppress a bad review or lose the paper until evening. Unluckily, he had them all sent by an agency and she did not often succeed. She always said, however, that nobody went by that paper.... She never praised a writer who was younger and more famous than himself. She was conveniently blind if envelopes arrived addressed in his own writing. She always saw that his room was left properly untidy—all except the flowers, which must never show the slightest sign of age. She came to avoid the word "reliable" and after six months never once split an infinitive at meals. Hubert at such moments would throw down his knife with a grimace of pain. He said it was a physical sensation, like cut corks, and spoilt his appetite, which she could never understand. And sometimes if it happened early in the day, she found at night that she had spoilt his work as well....

Such was the routine of Hubert Brett, ex-bachelor at thirty-five and writer of repute; all sacred and to be taken as an earnest matter—even that half-hour wherein he Kept In Touch With Modern Movements.

Helena learnt this, too, early.

There had been great excitement in the suburb after lunch. An aeroplane had passed upon its way to Hendon, and passed very low. The noise had been colossal, like six motorcycles. Every one, used as the place was to aeroplanes, had dashed out to the garden—every one but Hubert. Helena, even in her disappointment, could admire his self-restraint.

He seemed quite ignorant about it, too, when she made jokes upon the noise, as they set out for their tramp on the Heath.

"What time about?" he said. "Before lunch?"

"Why, Hugh," she laughed. "You must have heard! It sounded like a motor having its teeth drilled."

"No," he said. "I shouldn't have missed that. It is a sound I've never struck!"

She thought a moment. "Why, I know," she said. "You wouldn't have heard. Of course it was just after two and you were still keeping in touch with the movements."

To her surprise he stopped short, and looking up, she saw his cheeks were flushed below the eyes.

"My dear girl," he said pompously. "I enjoy your humourous way of looking at life, but it's a quite impossible position if a wife's going to be funny at the expense of her husband's ideals."

With which he strode onward and she fell in, a model wife, behind.

But she, of her simplicity, had meant it.

She had always admired his powers of concentration on those dull old literary weeklies. She had not even thought of sleep.

Every wife, perhaps, should be able to see through her husband the exact distance that he sees himself.

CHAPTER VI
GROWTH

Helena, when a year's passing had worn away the novelty of keeping house and made its process slower, was naturally rather bored at times, when Hubert was shut up with his work. No one could have been happier so long as she was with her husband; she still thought him immensely clever, which is most good for married happiness; still found their walks and treats the very greatest fun; but in the winter especially, there were so many gaps of idle loneliness.

Luckily the remedy was near at hand.

To a girl almost bursting with the ashamed desire for self-development a garden suburb must be Paradise indeed. There is a natural connection between New Art cottages with gardens round, and (let us say) enthusiasms. The ordinary man—that tame myope who gratefully accepts life as it is—contentedly exists in squares, crescents and straight lines; breathing the common air and never worrying at all whether his house, which may be number 246, has individuality or not. But the enthusiast, whom others call by a less noble title, is of a different sort. He holds that what we see and breathe, especially when young, we are. His children, then, must have a quite uncommon setting; not grown like the sordid brats in 245 "desirable villas" adjoining. No, they must live where there is air and a big back-yard patch; where the word garden throws a soft glamour over muddied and unfinished roads; where everything is beautiful and man himself is not so vile.

For, after all, he asks, what really wicked man would ever trouble to live out at a tube's end? No! Vice ever lurks among the fogs and shrubless rabbit-warrens of mid-London. It would not flourish in a garden suburb.

So out he goes, and sees to it that his house shall have something different from all the other small white dwellings round about him. An architect might say that there was neither use nor fitness in his timbered turret at the north-east corner, but he himself knows just why it is there. He knows that he has flung his little pebble, all he can avail, upon the heap that some day, we all hope, will crush the soul-destroying isms out of life, and make of man, not a type in monotone, but a great hive of multi-coloured individuals.

So far, so good; but more remains to tell.

He settles proudly underneath his turret and waits for the great change to start. The neighbours call and he discovers they are cultured. They are very cultured. And he—with a sick horror he knows at length that he is not. All these people here have something different, not a mere turret—something different about themselves. Menzies believes that eating sheep is murder in the sight of Heaven, and the same with cows. Du Cane will not let his children wear boots, because the notion is not Greek. Farren is convinced that you must sleep with your feet to the south and your head, of course, in the opposite direction. Blythe-Egerton believes in ghosts but says they can't have clothes. Jerningham lives next the golf club house, an envied site, and holds success in games has always been the first precursor of a nation's downfall. Escott knows exactly who should marry what; whilst Ferguson can quite explain the Post-Impressionists, but fails to understand the Royal Academy—peculiar in a Scotchman. Yes, every single one of them has some outstanding gift or knowledge, making him a pleasant man to meet.

So out he goes, post-haste, to search a quality, and wishes now that he had not spent all that extra money upon his symbolic turret. He knows a better secret, now, of how real individuality is gained. It consists not in bricks and mortar nor in any latticed garden-work—though these may be its outward signs—but in a being different. He hurries out and buys the works of Chesterton and Bernard Shaw as a beginning.

Helena, of course, was predisposed to it since Devonshire.

She did not long to become different, so much: she hankered to cease being ignorant.

Hubert was so clever, but that discouraged more than it helped her. He talked quite brilliantly about such deep things, but he would not explain. He laughed and said she was a jolly child. He always treated her rather as one and certainly they had great fun together, but she longed to be clever without getting old, and when she had told him so, he simply laughed and said she ought to be content to have such quaint ideas.

"It's far better," he added, "to be original than clever. Don't you worry your dear little head with dull ideas and facts."

But Helena did worry.

She had now, apart from her old desire for self-development and knowledge about life, all these dull lonely hours to fill; and as she went about, slowly getting to know the people near, she found like our enthusiast that every one of them was full of something—some vital, all-absorbing topic, if nothing more than golf or their own handicap. And that, she saw at once, was what she had to have if she wished ever to make her life really full. She could not go to matinées, like some, or Hubert missed her all the afternoon; and if they went to an At Home, he always dashed away at five, which looked so rude, and people—she felt sure—said afterwards that she could not have much hold over him, so soon. She tried novels, but these she really could not understand. Hubert watched cynically her attempts to get at grips with a sex-novel more sexual than is expected even in these days of censorships and free advertisement.

"But, Hubert," she said finally, "why did she do that? Wasn't she fond of her husband? He seems quite nice. Do these terrible things really happen?"

"Oh no," he answered, as one would speak to a child. "Of course they never happen really."

Helena looked puzzled. "Then why do people write or read them?" she asked.

"My dear girl," he answered in the heavy-father manner that gave him such pleasure, "if you could answer that, you would have solved one of the most interesting problems about human nature!"

So then she was puzzled again and laid aside the book half read, before she got even to the chapter that was really censured and commonly read first.

Not that way, she saw, lay illumination.

At last she tried another road. "You know," she said reflectively one night, during those long hearthside chats that neither really would have changed for any other social form, "I like all the people here and so on, but they're terribly busy, aren't they, and I always feel I've sort of come too late."

"How sort of?" he replied indulgently.

"Well, I've got no real friends and you're busy so much with your dull old work. Don't you know anybody?—really know, I mean—old friends, who aren't too far away?"

Hubert thought for a few moments. "It sounds absurd," he said at last, "but I was such a hermit till I met you that I don't believe I've got a single woman friend."

Helena, he noticed, was not flattered in the least degree. That sort of thing was what made her so splendid. He told himself that a woman who was womanly would be a bore about the house, and smiled adoringly on his own child-like specimen, who waited silently, as though quite sure that he would find a friend in the same way that after some time he had found her brooch. But there was a long pause and he made no suggestions.

"Well, what about men then?" she added simply. "I don't mind."

And he was once again enchanted by her naïveté.

"You shall have the pick of all my man-friends," he said, and then puzzled her by laughing.

"What is it?" she asked.

"Oh, you're so perfect, dearest!" he said, and got up and kissed her.

It needed some thought, none the less. Of his old pals—he suddenly remembered that he had been married over a year now, and not seen any one of them or wanted to—there were not many who lived near, and some of these ... well, they were all right in their way, but vaguely he felt they were not quite fit to introduce to any one so sweet as his girl-wife.... Marriage frequently turns cynics into sentimentalists. (The converse can be well ignored.)

"I know," he cried suddenly.

"I felt sure you would," she said. It was just these remarks that made her such an excellent companion. "Who is it then?"

"Old Boyd—old Kenneth Boyd. He's just the very man you'd like. One feels so awfully at home with him, he's restful you know; old-friend-in-five-minutes sort of fellow. Oh and," he added, "I forgot just for the moment! There is a wife too."

"I think I'm almost sorry," said Helena reflectively. "I don't think he sounds the sort of person who'd be much good unless alone. But I'm so silly with words. I never can explain and I expect I'm wrong."

There seemed, at any rate, some wisdom in her cryptic estimate.

The dinner-party was not a success.

Helena was so charming to Kenneth Boyd that Hubert, almost beyond himself with pride and refraining with difficulty from kissing her when she was too especially delicious, wondered why on earth he had so long delayed showing his old friends how sweetly original a little simpleton he had secured in spite of all their jeers. Kenneth, over a glass of port from the local grocer, was absolute enthusiasm and delighted his host till he turned suddenly and said; "Now own that I was absolutely right?" With the wives, however, it was different. Mrs. Boyd said afterwards to her husband: "Just the poor little undeveloped fool one would expect any one so conceited to take as his wife!" whilst Helena thought her a rude pig, and neither was too subtle in concealing her opinion.

This instinct of hostility was fatal to any real union between the households. Hubert noted with amusement how, at each fresh encounter, the two wives became more and more affectionately cold, and soon kissed on meeting.

He turned, with Helena still urging him, to other possibilities.

It was then that he thought of Geoffrey Alison.

"Geoffrey Alison," exclaimed Hubert with far more conviction than about Kenneth Boyd. "He really *is* the man! Amusing, clever, full of energy, and too young to be really busy." This in a condescending way.

"Why, how old is he?" she enquired. "I want some one, you know, who is cleverer than me and can tell me things at galleries and places."

He smiled at her. "Well, I think he could tell you things, he must be twenty-nine by now. Besides, I was able once to do him a good turn, he is a sort of protégé; so he'd be only too glad to take you about and as you call it, tell you things at galleries and places. He's pretty good on art."

The word protégé was rolled upon his tongue; the episode of Geoffrey Alison had pleased him a good deal; but Helena did not seem reassured.

"Oh, thank you!" she said, girlishly for these days when she had begun duly to expand as wished. "If he'd think he was doing it as a great favour, just to pay you back, I'd rather look at pictures and things by myself and puzzle out their meaning. It's only I've begun so late." She paused for a moment, and then without enthusiasm, almost sulkily; "What did you do for him?"

Hubert embarked on it with gusto.

"Why, it wasn't really very much. It was just after my first book came out, when I was twenty-six or so and he was at the Varsity or somewhere. I suppose he read a notice or heard the book was selling or something. Anyhow, he wrote me a most charming letter, the first I ever had from any stranger, congratulating me on my success and asking, if you please, how I had managed it as he heard I was young and he wanted to become an author too! I answered all the usual stuff about hard work and so on, which I see now he must have thought astounding twaddle if he really was at Oxford, and told him when he came to Town I'd like to meet him and perhaps could give him a few introductions. As a matter of fact," he went on after brief reflection, "I never did the last because I don't believe in it; but he came round at nights and talked to me and always said I had encouraged him a lot just when a little bucking-up was needed."

"And did he?" was Helena's sole comment.

Hubert at times could not follow her mind, fledgeling though it was, in all its flights. "Did he what, dear?"

"Why, did he become an author?" answered Helena, with that impatient tolerance which women keep for these occasions.

"Oh no," he said, vaguely annoyed, now, that he had not guessed it. "Rather not! He's an artist now. Not terribly successful, you know, but getting along. I don't think you would care much for his pictures, though."

Secretly, within his mind he reconstructed Alison, remembering now some not too pleasant drawings that he had brought along one night; wondering if he had mentioned him too soon. But he saw only a keen, harmless youth of the artistic type; a white man, certainly, who, even if he had a morbid side, would never show it to a girl—or to his benefactor's wife.

Yes, it was excellent. He had feared sometimes that she must be lonely in the mornings or from five to seven, and Alison, he knew, was of the work-when-I-feel-in-the-mood brigade (yes, it had certainly been Oxford), for he had finally been forced to tell him he was absolutely never free till after dinner-time.

He was the very man indeed. He spent his days in galleries, museums, theatres; wanted not only something new, like the Athenians, but every blessed new thing going; and if a heretic therefore on Art, was full of knowledge and when he cared to, could be very nice.

Helena thought him very nice indeed.

Of course he was ever so much cleverer than she was; she need not have feared that; and yet he did not seem to mind how elementary the thing was that she wished to see. He came with her and would explain it all. And he was nearly always free. Hubert had said that he was too young to be busy, and yet she felt slightly puzzled. If Geoffrey Alison could be so nice to friends, of whom he must have several, it did seem odd that Hubert never could afford a morning for his wife, when he had only one! But maybe Mr. Alison had not got many friends as yet or wasn't as nice to them all?

At any rate life up at Hampstead was far less boring now. Sometimes on days when there was not much house-keeping to do, they would go by tube or 'bus to Trafalgar Square and spend long hours in the National

Gallery or twenty minutes in the Tate to see the Watts room and three of the statues. At other times they would just ramble on the Heath, and prim Mrs. Herbertson, the vicar's wife, amused Helena one day enormously by thinking Mr. Alison was Hubert.

"Oh, I'm so sorry, dear Mrs. Brett!" she exclaimed, when Helena laughingly told her the mistake; "but seeing you two about upon the Heath so often in the mornings, I quite thought— —! You must forgive my stupidity, please?" And she smiled a false smile.

Helena thought this delicious, considering that Hugh was tall and broad and dark and looked like a celebrity at once, whilst Mr. Alison was rather short and slim, not one half so good-looking—funny-looking, somehow, even when quite serious—with fair hair always a wee bit too long!

"Won't Hugh be convulsed?" she asked.

"I don't think I should tell him," he said, to her absolute surprise.

"But why on earth not?" she enquired.

He would not tell her. In other things he was so kind; unlike her husband, he would try to fill her gaps in education; but here he was quite firm. He only let her force him to say that Hubert was a splendid fellow but a curious sort of devil—which she had learnt already, although she did not think that Mr. Alison should say so. He added that you never knew. And finally she gave it up, quite angry.

But she said nothing to her husband and Mrs. Herbertson might easily have made the same mistake again, except that she learnt Hubert was not a church-goer—an atheist, she called him—and cut Helena entirely. This left the young couple free, without social remorse, to make the most wonderful excursions on Hubert's one free day. All Sunday; the afternoon walk; mealtimes; after dinner—such was what Hubert gave her, and for the rest, always half-conscious of his selfishness, he felt delighted to think whilst working that Helena would not be bored. She was so busy, dear little simpleton, with this chimæra of her education!

It was Geoffrey Alison who first took her to causeries and lectures (she learnt almost at once to recognise a causerie, because the seats cost more), which took place at the Institute, conveniently after tea. Surprisingly good men came down—or up?—to speak, and spoke on a variety of subjects. Helena, always too nervous to air her knowledge before Hubert who was so clever and looked upon her (she knew) as a child, gradually began to juggle chaotically in her brain with such terms as Ethics, Syndicalism, Molecules, Collectivism, and Eugenics. It was all most difficult, she told herself, but frightfully worth while.

"Odd of her, this thirst for culture, isn't it?" said Hubert smilingly to Kenneth Boyd, on one of their rare meetings away from the hostile wives; "but it's quite harmless and it keeps them quiet."

Kenneth Boyd spoke gloomily. "Not always," he said. Perhaps he knew more of Woman, even though he never wrote about her. "Sometimes it has the opposite effect."

"Oh, I know what you mean," Hubert replied, not caring to be patronised; "but Helena is not that sort. She doesn't want the Vote. She's such a charming little innocent," and he laughed, half love but half pity.

"Really?" said the enigmatic Boyd. His thoughts had taken a far ampler sweep, and he spoke almost darkly.

Hubert did not answer. He was still thinking of the Vote. Most men persistently whittle down Woman's whole platform to a mere splinter convenient for smashing.

"Why," he elaborated, "if she were given it, she wouldn't know what she had got to do with it."

CHAPTER VII
THE CULT OF USELESSNESS

Helena certainly had small ambition towards the life political, even as anything no more exalted than a latch-key voter. She had been compelled to read politics in Devonshire but like a schoolboy who is forced to chapel, found it very dull, and took another course at the first opportunity. She could not think, she said, to Hubert's joy, how grown men even took the trouble of electing members who had no influence over their own party and spent most of the time in childishly hindering the other.

She did, however, wish to gain her self-respect.

She met, now, people vastly cleverer than those who had made her feel ignorant at home, so that her growing knowledge in no way kept pace with her aspirations. Those old vague yearnings for something which she used to call Being Herself were stronger now and in a form more definite. She had learnt, in the first year of her married life, all that a woman could learn about keeping house, but she still felt a fool. She knew that this was not enough for her, whatever it might be for others. She still loved to hear Hubert talking when he embarked on Art or some really big subject; but she wished to do more than listen.

And she was learning, too.

Those who give their time to that most wonderful and noblest of all trades, the making of a man, have lately come by the belief that children have been taught quite wrongly. They have been stuffed with knowledge before their bodies were grown to receive it. A deluge of facts has been poured upon them, seated at their little desks, and most of it has gone out through the open window into God's fresh air, where they ought to have been themselves. They have almost burst with learning—and never learnt to learn. They have known all Euclid at thirteen: forgotten everything by thirty-one. They have been specialists at seventeen and city clerks at twenty-three.

Mrs. Hallam, that crusted theorist and advocate of the old way, unconsciously had done a curiously modern thing. She had kept her daughter back, given her a healthy body, a mind anxious to expand and able. Now, at twenty-two, Helena began to specialise—in learning and in life. She had been kept back: now she leapt forward the better.

Contemptible enough perhaps to a superior eye, the salad of quite disconnected lectures, random talks with a young artist-friend, and pencilled passages from Mudie books, that formed this home curriculum; but as in health, contentment, as with life itself, the will to be is almost everything, and Helena was quite resolved to learn.

Her sole worry, in all the excitement of this onward surge into a fuller life whose endless spaces thrilled and terrified, was that her husband would not bear her company. Oh, he was much too clever. She knew that. She never blamed him. He had no need for all her causeries and things. She would be dull to argue with; and yet— —

Yet it is only human, only feminine, when one has got a clever husband and is adventuring on the long road of Art, to wish that he should take one's hand.

And she was proud of him.

Her simple mind had not yet probed the inwardness of Mrs. Herbertson's "mistake." It did not seem peculiar to her that Mr. Alison should be seen always, and he only, as her companion at the Institute. It merely was that she wished it might sometimes have been Hubert. She longed to hear his views on all of it, and it would be nice, too, to show him. It looked so odd that he would never come, when quite old-looking women brought husbands triumphantly along!

At length, when fifteen months of lectures gave her a new confidence, she tackled him point-blank one afternoon while they were walking on the Heath.

He looked at her reproachfully, as though he were a master who had just been asked for a half-holiday.

"My dear girl," he said, "is that quite logical?"

She knew at once that hope was dead. It always was when logic once appeared. She never had a chance.

"I don't know why not," she said gaily, for nowadays she did not go back to her kennel quite so easily. They had been married for two years.

Hubert was forced to put the thing in words.

"Well you see, my dear," he started, slowly, "I dare say other husbands have got their work finished by six o'clock. In fact"—and he brightened visibly—"that is really why they fixed that hour, I dare say. City men are back. But it's my best work-hour, you know."

"*Is* it?" laughed Helena, and looked at him. Then, as he did not seem to see the joke, "The *morning* is, you know, if I ask you to come out shopping. I'm afraid, Hugh, you're just a little naughty!" And she shook her finger.

"No," he said shortly, still not very much amused, for once, at her nice childish ways. "They *both* are.... It's not much for a man to work, just two short goes at it, and I simply can't spare the time, however much I'd like to. I mustn't go out between tea and dinner when I'm on a book."

"You used to, though," persisted Helena, "in Devonshire."

It is a rash wife who recalls to her husband the days of single life.

"Very likely," he answered impatiently; "but we weren't married then. I can't afford it now."

The rash wife had it, full between the eyes; a brutal blow provoked by her incaution; and she reeled.

"Can't afford it, Hugh?" she repeated, with a vague sense of being accused. "Why, do I cost so much? Do I cost more than Ruth?"

He had not looked for anything quite as direct as that. He had blurted it out and now, as often, felt ashamed. He laughed and said in a much kinder tone:

"Don't you worry your dear head about things like that. We shall be all right. You won't find the man in possession by our fireside yet, when you come home from market!"

Now it was her turn not to be amused. "No, but tell me," she said. "I'd much rather know. Are we honestly hard up?"

"What a practical little thing it's getting," he said, patting her on the back as they strode onward, always heralded by the long white dog with its straight tail, as proud as a drum-major. "Well, if you really want to know," he went on, "we are and have been, but we shan't be. Listen!" He turned about and about, his finger to his mouth, upon the empty spaces, clearly once more in the best of spirits. "Never tell a soul—and least of all the High-Art Alison—but I am doing a pot-boiler!"

"What, something worse than you need?" she blurted out in her astonishment.

He laughed at that. "Yes, if you put it so! Anyhow, something to make money."

"But won't the critics hate that?" she asked seriously.

Hubert Brett, for a man who had been almost too kindly reviewed, was always very hard on critics.

"Now listen," he said, "and I'll tell you something. The public has a natural suspicion of literary criticism. It only reads the stuff to see what to avoid. If it sees some book is called sincere, painstaking, artistic, a masterpiece, or anything like that, it passes on until it comes to something labelled crude and elementary. Then it gets out its library list. Think of the two best-selling novelists to-day, and then think what the critics say of them! They are a journalistic joke. Yes, the more the dear critics hurl abuse, the more the darling public rushes out to Boot's. I'm sick of good reviews and rotten sales. I'm not doing it because I married you, not I; but I want columns of abuse and half a million copies!"

She loathed it, always, when he talked like this. She never knew quite what he meant. She hoped he was not really writing a pot-boiler.

"No, but honestly," she said, "why are things worse than in the old days? Your books sell just as well. Do tell me or I shall ask Ruth."

"Well," he said, but this time without rancour, merely telling her what she had asked, "you see a house, even a hen-run like ours, always costs ever so much more than rooms—rates and things like servants, don't you see—and then Ruth used to make a bit with curious bazaar stuff all gummed on to tins."

It was a mere backwash of his thought, as he drew the question out to a solution—nothing more. He never thought of a comparison. Why, if the thing had ever come to that, Helena had her allowance....

But it went home to her, whose early days had bred a diffidence to die only with the years. Ruth had helped him, then!

"I wish I could do something," she said. "I feel so useless!" She had forgotten her bold attack with which this dialogue had started, and her whole mind was filled now with its self-reproach.

Hubert felt a sudden shame. The words threw back his memory to those first hours in London when the vast City crowd had made her say; "It makes me feel so useless!" Dear little girl, what happy, jolly days she had brought to his life since then! And yet she thought that she was useless....

She seemed so upset. His one idea was consolation. She must not think he longed for Ruth again, in even one respect!

Perhaps at a less flustered time he might have thought of all that she did in the house; those charming little meals, hot always at however variable times; the pretty bowls of flowers; everything so dainty—green and white—so different from the grimy lodgings.

But now he did not think of that. He took her arm instinctively in his and spoke what came into his mind.

"Dear little girlie," he said kindly, "I love you to be useless."

But she was not consoled.

CHAPTER VIII
A SCENE IN THE HOME

Hubert Brett could never quite escape from business; he analysed himself too much. His action sprung from impulse, education, ancestry, whatever source philosophers may choose to say, but it was followed by a sequel due to his own introspection. He tended in this way to set up something like a chain—a sequence of states which might almost be expected after any given act.

He might have owned, found in a candid vein, that selfishness was his besetting fault. It had been so—this would be his excuse, if he indeed admitted what certainly he knew—it had been so from birth; at any rate since he recalled himself an only son and younger than his only sister, pampered and indulged so far as even a small child could wish. He always *had* got what he wanted. Hence naturally sprang a sort of self-centredom, a tendency to think first of what *he* desired, something which, well, hang it all, no, it wasn't selfishness, but merely that self-confidence which all men who meant to get things done must first of all possess....

None the less, every now and then (he noticed it more, since Helena had been with him), he did, he knew, do things no doubt quite justifiable if one were thinking only of success, efficiency, and so forth; but rather beastly from the other person's—from Helena's—standpoint. It was so easy, when defending your own interests (and otherwise you'd get no work done ever), to be thoughtless, irritable, mean.

About those lectures or whatever they were of the poor little girl's, for instance....

Ought he, came the doubt when he was back in his own den at one minute past five o'clock—ought he to have given in to her for once, if she was really so immensely keen to take him? After all there often were days when he had finished work easily by six o'clock; whole months, even, between books, when he did no work after tea; but there was such a thing as System, and though a married man, he was quite bachelor enough to love this time of solitude with pipe and books. Helena was sweet; no man could ever have been luckier about his wife; but he saw her for much more than one-half the day and all of it on Sundays.

Yes really, he could not see that she had any right to look for more. Perhaps those City men took their wives to these precious causeries, but they were ever so much more away. Oh yes, he saw a lot of her and however much she might complain, he knew that she was really lucky....

All the same, as he never had and the dear child wanted it, perhaps——?

Whereat Hubert, having worked comfortably around his usual circle— Selfishness, Remorse, Ample Self-Excuse, and Noble Expiation—got up, feeling very light of heart, and went back to the drawing-room.

Helena was startled. She never thought of tragedies, she had known none in her well-sheltered days, or she might easily have feared that there was something wrong. Never in these two years and more had he come back, once gone, till dinner-time. Many modern wives might have resented such a sudden entry. Luckily this specimen was in no more compromising a position than that of eating the last jam sandwich, a thing she never could resist before Lily came and took away the tea. She waved it at him without shame.

"Hullo!" she said. "Why what's brought you back?"

He smiled indulgently. He liked her to be young.

"Look here, Helena," he said, "I've been feeling I was a bit of a brute about those causeries of yours. I could easily spare an evening some day, if you'd like me to. Let's see the list and then we'll fix on one."

Many modern wives, again, might have been tiresome about an amende honourable indeed but so obviously planned. Not Helena, however. She leapt to get the circular, all thrilled excitement and babbling gratitude.

Hubert ran a proud finger down the list. "Hullo," he said in unflattering surprise. "They've got some quite good men."

He had always utterly ignored her ventures in self-education. He did not, for one thing, approve of them; and he had vaguely thought they were connected with the parish church, Pleasant Sunday Evenings, and everything like that.

"I'm so glad you're pleased," she put in, quite without irony.

"That's the one we'll do together," he said, and read out—"'January 29: Art as a Religion.—G. K. Shaw.' And only ten days off, too!"

It was the best, far, on the list; he would perhaps be called on, as a local author, to make some remarks; and he might meet the lecturer....

"Oh, but how splendid!" she cried, duly grateful. "Just the very one I wanted you to come to. You really *are* a dear! And that's a late one too, at eight o'clock, because the lecturer objected, so your old work won't suffer after all!"

She talked of it for days to come, what great fun it would be, till Hubert felt even more guilty. He had never realised how much she felt the fact of his not coming. He had not ever heard, you see, dear Mrs. Boyd say: "What! No husband again? I don't think you keep him in at *all* good order; does she, Kenneth?" —as one who should say, "You have no power over him, at all!" He did not guess how lonely she had felt sometimes when Geoffrey Alison could not escort her. Still he saw her great keenness now and told himself he would have gone to these lectures before—if only he had known they were not University Extension.

He was distinctly flattered by the way she harped upon this small concession. Little things like that had a curious power of making Hubert Brett well satisfied with life.

She could see that afresh, six mornings later.

He was opening his letters, a process which made breakfast quite a nervous time for her, because one small reverse—no more than an unflattering review—upset him so and sometimes ruined his whole morning's work, which meant he would be silent and depressed at lunch-time.

To-day, however, having opened first the only letter in an unknown hand as promising the most adventure, he said with real exhilaration:

"Ah, that's encouraging. That bucks one up!"

"What, good news, Hugh dear?" she inquired, delighted.

"Yes, the Kit Kat Club has asked me as its guest of honour."

Inwardly she was a little disappointed; she had hoped it would be some money.

"How excellent!" she said, good wife; and then, "What *is* the Kit Kat Club?"

"Why, it's a well-known literary club," he answered, slightly hurt. "They meet" —he read the card again—"at Lewisham."

"Capital!" she said: not because she had ever heard of Lewisham as a great literary centre, but because he was so terrifically pleased. "And when is it to be?"

"Very short notice," he said, looking once more at the invitation. "This very Tuesday, January 29th. Lucky we never dine out!"

"But Hugh," she began, oh so disappointed, and then stopped. She had told every one—well, Mrs. Boyd—that she was bringing Hugh this time....

He understood. "Why, it's the lecture or debate," he said. "I *am* sorry." There clearly was no question which should go. Then, much more gently, remembering her keenness: "Never mind, little girl: we'll find another nice debate. Let's see the list and we will pick one now."

Treats, of course, are seldom a success the second time. Helena, now, did not dash for the list. In fact Hubert, looking up, saw that great tears were rolling down her cheeks.

She could have killed herself for shame. It only proved how difficult it was to be grown up, if you began too late!

And Hubert was not even touched by it. The silly action had no sanction in success.

He got up angrily, without a word, but making it clear that he had thought her selfish. He sat on the armchair and took up the *Spectator*. This announced that breakfast was now over.

Helena felt that his rebuke was thoroughly deserved. What must he think of her, when they took place each week and he had offered to come to another? Of course he didn't know about that rude pig, Mrs. Boyd!

"Hugh dear," she said, also getting up, "I am so sorry; I feel such a beast. It's only I was disappointed. Of course my meeting's simply nothing. I ought to have been glad about the Kit Kats, and I am."

Some men, after that, would possibly have changed their minds and taken her to her dear meeting; but to Hubert nothing came before success.

"That's a dear unselfish little wife," he answered soothingly and gave her a forgiving kiss. The episode was closed.

"You're sure it is the twenty-ninth of this month?" she therefore angered him by asking. Helena could not believe in Fate being so brutal.

"Well, there's the card," he answered brusquely.

She took it up, filled with an abrupt, unchristian desire to tear it into fragments. It had a silly black cat in silhouette upon it and she *had* thought he would come at last....

"Why Klub with a K?" she did allow herself to ask.

"Just a literary conceit, I suppose," he answered, trying to control his voice; and that silenced her, because she had no theories as to what a literary conceit might be.

But Hubert could not quite allow the matter to rest there. He felt that she was thinking he had acted selfishly and he must prove to her that everything would be all right. What odd disguises can Remorse assume!

"You can get Alison to take you," he threw out. "He's sure to be going."

"Oh no," answered Helena. "I told him you were coming. He'll be booked. No, I shan't go at all."

Face Mrs. Boyd exultant? No, not she. Afterwards, if needed, some excuse. But anyhow not that! She had said she was bringing Hubert.

"That's silly, my dear." He did not often call her that. "Alison will take you gladly, I know, or if not you can go alone. You often have before."

"Yes," she retorted, "but not when I've told every one that you were taking me. I have a little pride."

He shut his paper and got up. He never could bear scenes.

"Just as you like," he said, trying to speak evenly. "It's your concern. I was only thinking of your comfort. Whatever you do won't hurt *me*."

A man can escape everything except himself; and so it chanced that Hubert Brett felt a brute twice, repented twice, about one causerie.

He felt it most acutely in his little room.

He very nearly went back to her now, a second time, and said so; but then he remembered what a nasty scene it had been, about nothing. Of course in the old anti-marriage days it had been his pet theory that every wedded pair inevitably—by force of Nature, which meant every one to dwell apart—ended in continued rows; but it had seemed so quite impossible with Helena. Perhaps it always did!...

So sweet and pliable and ignorant of life she had been—yes, this was a new Helena and more like the old Ruth!

No, he would not go back.

He would be hanged if he encouraged her.

CHAPTER IX
CINDERELLA

Helena tried not to look as though she minded when Hubert came down, glorious in evening dress at six o'clock.

"It *is* an early start," she said cheerfully.

"Yes," he replied; "but that means I shall be home all the earlier. The dinner begins at seven and I shan't make a long speech—trust me—so you can expect me back not later than half past ten or eleven at the very latest."

He just restrained himself from saying once more that he thought her stupid not to go across to the Institute instead of moping all alone till then. Even so his farewell was a little cold for, though he kept silence, he could not help feeling she had been selfish over the whole business. Her air of martyrdom had rubbed some gilt off the occasion's splendour.

As for Helena, having waved him gaily out of sight, she did not return and give way to a natural sorrow, as he imagined, typically penitent so soon as he had parted from her. She looked, it is true, hard and thoughtful for a moment. Then she laughed almost happily. What did it matter really? It would only be one evening alone, one lecture missed;—and who was Mrs. Boyd? Why of course any one really nice would be glad that her husband had been honoured by these beastly Kit Kats, whoever they might be.

She sat down and wrote a long letter—about everything else in the world—to her lonely mother, who after all never had any one at all to dine with her, unless you counted clergymen.

That finished, it was dinner-time and that was fun because she had ordered or brought in all her pet kickshaws—shrimps, dough-nuts and so forth—which Hubert always vetoed, describing them expansively as dirty feeding. Men, she decided, got so little out of life; always beef and cabbages and yesterday to-morrow....

It was really quite a philosophic meal. She often was alone, for some big part indeed in every day, but there was something in this first lonely dinner that made a curious break and gave, as the French say, to think. She thought of her old life in Devonshire; she thought of her ambitions towards self-development when she decided upon marriage; she thought without pride of herself as she was at present; and she thought of Hubert.

She had reached the dough-nut course, and also the conclusion that they were an odd couple but probably most couples were, when the front door bell sounded, as it always did, through the whole little house.

Helena looked at the clock. Ten minutes to eight! No parcel-post. What could it be, possibly? Not Hubert back? She felt a quick shame of the dough-nut.

It was beneath the table safely before Lily entered.

"Please'm," said the maid, "it's Mr. Alison wants to speak to you."

Helena went out into the hall. "Hullo," she said, hoping he had not expected dinner. "Have you been to the Institute? What was it like?"

"Been," he laughed. "No! It's only ten to eight. This is an eight-o'clocker, you know. G. K. S. will never stand things at the ordinary time!"

This was a blow. Helena, not letting herself think of all that she was missing, had yet fancied that it was safely over. And it had not even begun... "Oh," was all that she said.

"I went along," Geoffrey Alison proceeded quickly, as though every instant counted, "because I am a steward so had to be early, and asked just out of curiosity where you were sitting. They said, so to speak, you weren't! I knew you both intended coming so I ran across. I've got two tickets just returned, so if— —"

"How very kind of you," said Helena, feeling that she could almost slay him; "but it wasn't that we couldn't get in. Hubert at the last moment found that he wasn't free, so we sent our seats back. He suddenly remembered he was dining out." She tried to make it sound as though there had not been a tiff.

"Dining out?" repeated Geoffrey Alison, "Well then, you're free to come along like all the other ones?"

"Oh no, thank you; I don't think I will," said Helena. She had not forgotten about Mrs. Boyd.

"But you simply *must*," replied the other, pulling out his watch. "They'll be beginning if we don't make haste. You couldn't miss this possibly; it's far the best of the whole series. Old Dr. Kenyon, too, thinks art is a disease and intends asking questions. It will be tremendous. Come along or you will make us late."

"But I'm not tidy or anything," said Helena. Definite objections are the first steep steps down from refusal to complaisance.

He recognised this. "So much the better," he cried in prompt triumph. "Unprepared things are always the best sport. You don't need wraps; it's like a summer night and you look very smart. Come on! Your husband won't object. It will be simply grand. We'll have a picnic causerie!"

Helena was swept away. Bother Mrs. Boyd and every one! It really would be fun and she would be so bored at home. Hubert had told her she should go. Besides—did she feel dimly, ever so little even, that she was somehow getting even with him? Let us pass quickly on, with all the charity that we can muster....

The Institute was packed. This was clearly a great night.

Helena, directly she entered the room, full of an excitement that had almost the sensation of magnetic waves, was glad that she had come. And as they found their seats, the chairman and the speaker entered.

That evening, as Mr. Alison had promised, was the jolliest of the whole of the series. She even enjoyed merely looking at this G. K. Shaw.

He was ever such a big man, who swelled genially outward and then ended unexpectedly in quite a savage beard. He looked so comfortable and friendly that she felt certain all the nice things he meant to say (you could tell from his eyes) got somehow twisted all wrong in that horrid beard.

Certainly, to judge by mere words, there was a lot with which she could not sympathise and some she could not understand. If only Hubert had been free!

He said, for instance, that conventional Religion was man's excuse to the Almighty: that faith was the power of believing what we could not prove untrue: and that churches should possibly be built, because of unemployment, but left empty for the glory of their Maker. All this puzzled her, and Mr. Alison would only chuckle, while most others grunted. Then the lecturer got round to Art and said that life was the Creator's masterpiece. He roughly defined Art as that which never found its way to paper. He admitted the existence of a body of literature and paintings. He did not for a moment wish to conceal the existence of the Royal Academy. One corn-crake, however, did not cause a winter: and he wished to-night to speak only about Art. The modern out-look was parochial and men failed to see even the parish for looking at the clergymen. An Artist had no fatherland. He had the key of the World: for paint was thicker than blood. No two nations had ever agreed on armaments or treaties: but all admitted that Farnese was greater than Phil May. The worry with the world to-day was not that it was old: it was a million years too young. No man troubled with the future, because he knew that it must some day be the past. Religion hinted at the future: Art alone interpreted the present. Five thousand years had thrown mud at the workman: Brangwyn proved him the sole dignified thing left in a dead-level age. For centuries they had destroyed old ruined tenements, and Bone had shown them to be the only kind that ought to be allowed. Art dealt with the beautiful and live; the Church with what was gloomy and decayed. You could not make people wicked by Act of Parliament; the plain man was an artist when he shaved his face. Art was to the English what death had been to the Egyptians, but London was full of things that no one ever spoke about. There was, for instance, the Imperial Institute. It was better to be beautiful than dead. Some of those he met were neither. He wished that they were both. He should be glad if any one would raise objections, for their mutual advantage. Every one was right and nobody was ever wrong.

There had been ever so much more than that, she knew; but this was all she could recall when finally he took his seat, and now, already, she was not altogether sure how it had been connected. She was not by any means convinced but she was tremendously encouraged. New vistas of an unsuspected length and freshness opened out from a drab world, whilst the fat, bearded man was speaking. Sometimes she supposed he must be very funny?

"Capital, capital," murmured Mr. Alison, and only that. He usually had such a lot to say, too! She was disappointed.

But now grimly and deliberately there uprose an elderly man of stern broad face and a respectable frock-coat. He must apologise for letting his heavy periods drop on the top of the last speaker's brilliant flippancies, but truth, he regretted to say, was truth.

"That's old Kenyon," her neighbour whispered gleefully.

The doctor, having said so much of calm preface as due to a visitor, suddenly blazed out into a quicker time and a more violent mood. So far, he said, from Art being a religion, it was a disease. (Sensation.) He proved this at some length, largely in the dead languages, with extracts read from small pamphlets which (he announced) he had the honour to have contributed to various of the famous Monthlies.

The soldier-type, he argued, was the most essentially male, 'and it was furthest-moved from the artistic. He went so far, in conclusion, as to say that literary creation was only possible to a hybrid creature half-male and half-female, of whichever sex.

The general feeling was that this was rude to Mr. G. K. Shaw.

The famous author rose, however, blandly and swung his body round to Dr. Kenyon.

"Now there'll be some fun," said Geoffrey Alison.

"I consider," said Mr. G. K. Shaw quite gravely, holding his beard steady, "that the last speaker's mongrel theory of literature is plausible and valuable. I am, however, puzzled as to how he accounts for his own admirable pamphlets?"

Which certainly was fun and everybody laughed, to the annoyance of old Dr. Kenyon, who was thenceforth nicknamed "Mongrel" and shortly after moved to Wimbledon.

But beyond all this, Helena found a vague excitement in the evening. It was not like those other causeries at six o'clock; she wished they always could take place at eight. The mere fact, too, of having come so on the moment's spur lent quite a new attraction. As Geoffrey Alison had hinted, picnics are more romantic than a dinner-party and this had bulked into almost an adventure.

He saw her home. The speeches had been long and it was half-past ten already, but all was darkness in the little house.

Helena had quite a feeling of nervousness at the idea of switching on light after light, alone. "Come along in," she said simply. "Hubert'll be here in half a moment. Then he'll give you a drink, and we will all exchange experiences!" All rancour had gone; yet—well, she would rather like to show Hugh that his absence didn't mean she merely sat and cried! Women *are* human—and women.

"No, I don't think I will, thanks very much," he said.

His face and tone puzzled her. "Don't say *you*'re busy, now!" she cried. "It's a regular disease."

"Oh no, I never work at night," he answered. "Artists can't very well. That is the one advantage of our job!"

"Well don't be tiresome then, and come on in," she said, holding the door open. "Hugh will be furious if he knows you're just gone. So don't be stupid. *I* was tame, just now!"

"If you really mean it," he replied almost solemnly and entered.

"Of course I do," she laughed. "Should I invite you, otherwise? How curious you are! Come into the dining-room and then when Hugh comes, he can give you—Oh no, let's come into here!" She hastily pointed to the drawing-room.

Geoffrey Alison went in, puzzled, thinking.

He did not know, and she had only just remembered, about that dough-bun.

CHAPTER X
HONOUR

Hubert meanwhile was enjoying quite another sort of artistic evening. On first arrival, indeed, at the Club (which proved to meet in a Hotel Coffee Room), he found himself wondering whether he might not have been wiser in keeping to the old arrangement. The Lewisham Kit Kats, on entry to their circle, did not promise so much intellectual reward as G. K. Shaw and the scorned Institute. They had not the exotic charm of their great prototype.

He had imagined, always, a band of young enthusiasts in Literature, fresh maybe from the 'Varsity, who would be glad to hear what he had got to say and welcome him to their—it might be—weekly dinner. But here were no evening suits except his own, of which he grew now only too aware. The common dress was dark suit, bow-tie, and moustache; or with the women—for it was "mixed"—what he imagined would be blouse and skirt. They were a frowsy-looking lot, he told himself; horribly genial; and he more than suspected them of being Bohemian. There was a tortured look of gladness upon every face. They bowed elaborately and shook hands with fervour, until the whole room buzzed with brotherly salutes. And Hubert, in his dress-suit, stood among them. One by one the members were brought up and all of them shook hands. Not one among the sixty who failed to be very proud to meet him. Hubert sighed for Helena and G. K. Shaw, finding his only means of consolation in elaborating it as a good story. He wished that he could say with truth that they had not an *h* among them, but this was not so. He would have liked them better, he decided, if that had been true. They were snobs in their own way, he felt confident, and their gentility was an affair of effort. They were that trying set, the in-betweens....

It was with genuine relief he heard that dinner was now served, and in they trooped: he first with his allotted woman; the rest, all apologetic smiles, falling in anyhow behind. They settled at the tables in a hungry silence. Hubert could see the waiters smiling at his evening dress,—or thought he could, which was equally unpleasant. He turned hurriedly to his neighbour, whose name he had failed to catch in his agitation. He only remembered the friendly President murmuring in his ear: "Her brother is a book-reviewer," as though that gave her a niche all apart.

"How often do you have these dinners?" he decided to begin.

She aimed a toothy smile straight at him. Hubert had never noticed how unusually fat she was before, and tried hard not to seem as though he had observed it now. He looked doggedly at her light yellow hair, and then looked down again when he saw that it was not real.

"I'm not a Kit Kat, you know, Mr. Hubert Brett," she answered coyly. "They meet every Tuesday, but we ladies are only asked when there is some special attraction, so you see you should feel very honoured! I find it most interesting" (she laid the accent upon the third syllable), "because you see, my brother is a book reviewer, so I naturally take a special interest."

"Naturally," answered Hubert.

"We always say," she went on, very animated, "just for a joke, you know, only among ourselves, that the Kit Kats have a far gayer time when we ladies are not admitted: we see them on their best behaviour!"

"Yes?" Hubert said absently, forgetting to smile or to live up in any way to this pet joke amongst the ladies. He was thinking. "What does your brother review for?" he enquired as a result.

The big lady looked on him a little sternly, not at all sure whether he had not intended to be rude. He had been very short with her pleasantry, and now was he doubting about Harold? He ought to know the name.

"For several books," she said with dignity, and turned to the man on her other side, who might not be a famous author but was the Mayor's cousin and far less stuck-up.

Hubert knew that he had failed, and his other neighbour proved unhappily to be deaf on the near side. He spent the rest of a long and essentially British meal in trying to appease the critic's sister. It was all rather difficult, and he was glad now that he had told the President he must leave early, as his wife was nervous and he had a long way to go. He could escape a little before half-past nine and they would be much happier without him. He wished now that he had refused the whole thing. Still, it *was* something to be chosen as the guest of honour....

And, indeed, when all the meal had gone except its odour and the President had facetiously announced that the ladies might now smoke, it proved to be a very big thing indeed to be the Kit Kats' guest of honour.

Even Hubert Brett's tried capacity for absorbing flattery was strained when Mr. President, as everybody called him always, spoke minute after minute in praise of his books: recalling their names (from a list propped up on his cigar-tray), although he was sure Kit Kats would not need reminding.

These sterling merits which he had just enumerated had won, he said, for Hubert Brett, if he might drop the Mr. in Art's fellowship (applause), a big following in Lewisham, and to-night's event, he felt confident, would render it yet bigger. Frankly, as President, when he thought of this fixture he had felt pleased. (Applause.) Of the distinguished novelist's affability in acceding to their desire in spite of the many calls upon his time and recent marriage (laughter), he intended to say nothing. (Some applause.) He here read out, he confessed with a certain pride, the names of distinguished authors who had so acceded formerly, and Hubert was half disappointed yet half flattered to find himself able to agree with the President's remark that none of them was so popular or well-known an author as their guest to-night. "He has told me," slyly concluded the orator, "that the trains home are bad and that his wife is sitting up for him. (Laughter.) Those of us who are married men will understand." (Loud laughter and a high-voiced "Shame," then female tittering.) "I only pull aside the veil in this way so as to let you realise why I draw my remarks short to-night and call upon our guest of honour, Hubert Brett, for the pleasure of a few words upon the literature of to-day, in which he plays so considerable a part."

Enormous applause greeted this conclusion and to it was added the clapping of white gloves (for all the ladies wore them), as Hubert rose and stood behind his chair. Even the lady whose brother reviewed, possibly melted by hearing that her neighbour was a genius to whom much always is forgiven, smacked him playfully on the back as he got up to speak.

He was not a good speaker and prudently had written out the headings of his speech and a few epigrams that might pass as impromptu after wine. There had not, unluckily, been any wine and all the early epigrams passed quite unnoticed. A speech devised for 'Varsity enthusiasts was not of the true Kit Kat bouquet.

Hubert had so far got the instincts of an orator that he could realise this fact. The chilly aspect of his listeners told him that he had not gripped them; a swift ranging back to the last speech supplied the cause. He was not broad enough in his effects. They did not care for theories on writing; they wanted something personal. They wanted reminiscences. Their welcome, when he first got up, had shown they took him seriously. Nobody of his own set was there! What harm?

Hubert Brett's speech (for no one ever used the Mr. of him afterwards) is still remembered as the most enjoyable of all the Kit Kats ever heard. Such interesting people had he met and known, known well; such vivid lights he threw upon the full life of a famous literary man.

No single member who got up to join in the discussion afterwards but started with an eulogy of their guest's work and speech.

Hubert was very pleased. He had warmed to the Kit Kat manner. He should not tell it as a comic story; it would not be fair. After all, perhaps they were not an artistic set, but then not everybody could belong to that, and they were very genial. You only had to get to know them. They were the Public anyhow, the class for whom one wrote, and possibly they might have influence, some few of them. This woman next door, now so affable, had got a brother who reviewed for several papers. All of this must help. It was absurd to be exclusive when one came to Art. He looked upon this evening as one of the most encouraging in his whole life. Wouldn't Helena be pleased to hear it all?

And that reminded him.

With a hot shame he drew out his watch.

His speech had been long and one of many after a full dinner. It was very nearly half-past ten and a long journey home....

Full of guilt, he pulled himself together, to make his excuses. There was a gap now. No one seemed to volunteer as speaker. He— —

But Mr. President was on his feet. He must not interrupt.

"Gentlemen—*and* Ladies!" said the President amid appreciative laughter, "all the volunteers now being exhausted, I shall proceed in accordance with Kit Kat tradition to call out the reserve and ask them to speak, whether they wish it or no. And the first gentleman I think we all feel we should like to hear speak is our old valued friend and excellent critic, Mr. Henry Jenks."

This met with such general applause that Hubert felt it would be ridiculous to get up now. It also would be rude and pointed. Besides, "critic"—did he mean professional? It might be silly to offend him. After all, these people who were asked to speak would surely be better, their estimate of his work more worth while, than those who simply wanted to hear their own voice?

Helena wouldn't mind. She was so easy-going, bless her. She would love to hear.

To the flattered relief of a vigilant President, who had observed the guest of honour's restless movement, Hubert settled once more in his chair.

He would stay ... just a little.

CHAPTER XI
PINK PAPERS AND ST. ANTHONY

It is both easy and comforting to divide men simply into opposites. Honest, dishonest; truthful, lying; clean, dirty;—what a lot of worry it undoubtedly prevents. You trust one person all the way, another nowhere; you tell your secrets to the first and to the second nothing; it is so simple that few people can resist it, when they come to life. And it is good enough for working purposes.

But in reality it is not so. A man all white or all black is but rarely met: the last is soon removed, the first impossible for common use. Man was devised from a more subtle palette; and if in all the millions of faces no two are alike, that is yet truer, said about the heart. The man you trust so freely has his see-saw moments, like anybody else, and if as a rule he lands the right end down, it may have been your very confidence that lent him weight. It is the same with all. They must be entered for convenience beneath the colour which they most display, but every one of them is a true moral rainbow and much more. Take it all in all, we humans are the most mixed thing that any one has ever yet invented: the reason why some scorn all other hobbies or amusements, so long as there is Man.

Geoffrey Alison was an especially odd mixture—all of course kept rigidly inside. To the mere eye he was, like most, quite simple, almost to the point of dulness. Oh yes; I see, yes; the artistic type; a gentleman though; trustworthy but slack; quite modest although jolly clever; pretty much of a white man... But inwardly he was a thing to watch because his types conflicted, and that ends with fireworks.

He joined the artist's soul—a real love for the beautiful and noble—to what perhaps may be most easily described as a pink-paper mind. He could sit and gaze happily for hours at a Corregio, forgetting the plush benches and the noisy tourists, utterly absorbed; he found a joy that was almost physical in a sudden landscape or the moon which breaks loose from its clouds and gleams on a rough sea; he would watch with a smile of pleasure the way of a woman with her child or a child with its toy; he shrank with loathing from all that was ugly, sordid—the sight of needless misery or the sound of a woman's oath; and yet—and yet he could not rid himself of the idea that there was something palpitating, wicked, spicy, about a shop-girl who held up her skirt to cross a muddy road. There was a thrill for him each time that he passed a stage-door. Garters—champagne (always known as fizz)—corsets—chorus girls—these all held for him a brimming measure of romance. He was convinced that there was something specially cryptic and alluring about bar-maids, though he would never enter bars as he did not like other people's glasses. Paris to him stood for a riot of continued orgies shaming a white dawn. He was of those who for peculiar reasons can thoroughly enjoy a really English ballet. The thought of studios and models had half consciously affected the choice of his career; and if he now knew that to be illusion, so far as his experiences went, he still liked—well, one half of him—to read the old exciting fairy-tales. Perhaps they happened somewhere, still.

At times, when he was on a holiday or anywhere except at his own news-shop, he would buy, half-ashamed and furtive, those strange, elemental papers whose main task it is to tickle the broad tastes of City youths or Army officers. And he thoroughly enjoyed them—until afterwards.

Army men, in fact, who had glared at him all through a long dinner-party, often revised their estimate when coffee had come in and their wives departed; if, be it understood, the conversation drifted into a right channel. On the way home, should their wives say; "I liked that Mr. Alison, so clever!" they would reply: "M'yes? Rather an affected ass, my dear: I can't stand those artistic johnnies. Still, he came out a bit over the wine and showed he *had* got something in him. Not a bad fellow I dare say; bit of a sportsman possibly—in spite of his long hair. But I'm not sure we want to have him calling?" Which only shows how useful it may be for any man to have two sides. You never can please all the world with one!

Of course the one in question was entirely abstract. Geoffrey Alison would never have even dreamt of doing all the things he liked to read on paper. It would perhaps have been more healthy if he had; but no, he realised, himself, that it was only an idea.

It was an idea, too, that he shared with no one. His friends—artists and authors—somehow were not amused by anything of that sort, although the papers he enjoyed were read by millions. It was curious! He kept it to himself, and that was bad as well. To Hubert he had raised the curtain for one moment, with those sketches of his own, but the audience had not seemed keen for more. And as for Helena—well, inwardly Geoffrey Alison was an odd mixture; but he remained a gentleman outside.

All the same, to-night was trying him a little hard.

Helena's friendliness had thrilled him from the day they met. He had never met a woman—anyhow not young and pretty—who had taken to him like that from the first. He never had regarded himself as a lady's man; he was too small and timid; yet she had seemed to find nothing wrong with him. She had adopted him as her guide and philosopher in art; gone about with him more, almost, than with that absurdly busy fellow Brett; until the cattish vicar's wife— —!

And now— —!

Of course he knew that she was just a girl, and jolly innocent and all that sort of thing (Brett liked to keep her back), but even so, any one surely would admit that it was a little bit exciting and peculiar. The way she asked him in; and then he could not make out why she changed her mind about the dining-room and came into the drawing-room where she sat down upon the sofa and looked simply ripping. It was all very odd!

Of course she was innocent and jolly, but he believed that she was fond of him and some day he would love—when they were all alone like this— if only half in fun—to give her just one kiss. She surely couldn't mind? It would be splendid and exciting. (It may be added that Geoffrey Alison thought more of its excitement than its splendour.)

The very idea made being with her like this so difficult and trying. He could not think of anything to say. It all sounded wrong.

Even Helena noticed, at last.

"How dull you are to-night!" she said peevishly, for they were old friends and she never troubled to sort out her words. "I believe you *did* want to work or else had something else to do."

"Of course not," he protested, feeling horribly wronged in the circumstances. "This is awfully jolly." Why couldn't he be natural?

Helena was not so confident about the jollity. "Hugh *must* be here soon," she remarked rather wearily.

"Why do you call him Hugh?" he asked, jumping at a topic. "Surely that's not really short for Hubert? It ought to be Bert!"

"Oh, how dare you?" she asked gaily; she felt that they had got back on to the old easy paths. "Bert indeed—for him! I wonder how you——" and she clapped her hands excitedly. "Yes," she said, her boredom all forgotten, "that's it! I always thought that Mr. Alison was far too stiff; I've got a name for you."

"For *me*?" That silly blood was jumping in his brain.

"Yes," she cried. "Ally! I shall call you Ally, just like Ally Sloper! That's better than Bert."

Ally. It was not romantic, no; but still——

Gad, what a ripping little girl she was!

He wished to goodness he hadn't ever thought about that kiss. He could have been ever so much more amusing, make her like him more, if only he hadn't got that possibility before him. And yet ... perhaps it was worth while.

But Helena had no such abstract thrill to keep her eyes open and it was well after eleven. She wished now that Mr. Alison had not come in. When Hubert got back, they'd sit and have drinks. She wished that he would go. And how she longed to yawn! If only he would even be amusing....

"Have you seen my snap-shot album?" she asked. In their two years of friendship, it had never come to this before.

"No," he said. "May I?" feeling very young. He knew that he was being entertained.

She leant down wearily to get it from the bookshelfs lower row. Her smooth white neck stretched in a rounded slope before him. By Gad! His hands moved restlessly towards her. This was his great chance. She might not even ever know!

And then—she was so innocent. Suppose she boxed his ears or anything like that? Supposing she told Brett?...

"No, don't worry with it," he said, finding it quite hard to speak. "I think I'd better go. It's too late for snap-shots! He must have missed his train."

"He'll be here any moment now," she felt compelled to say.

"I know," he answered meaningly, as though that explained his going. She did not notice of course, was just puzzled for a moment, but it gave him another thrill. As he passed through the hall, with her beside him, he saw the minute hand was nearer to midnight than to any other hour; a very dissipated time....

And outside, in the little garden, he drew a long breath, as though to set free the vanquished evil thoughts. He felt he had been very good to-night in face of opportunities for other things.

St. Anthony himself could not have felt much more complacent.

CHAPTER XII
DEVILS

Hubert groped his way homewards along the ill-lit road, filled by a certain shame but also nearly chuckling to himself.

What a splendid, encouraging night it had been! Those last and most important speakers were if anything even more enthusiastic about all his novels. It was nice to get into touch with those for whom you wrote and know that they are pleased. It took away the great drawback of a writer's job as compared with the vocalist's or actor's; that you never heard the clapping. (He did not, of course, think about the hisses.)

Wouldn't Helena be glad to hear it all!

He had forgotten by now that there had been any trouble as to this evening's fixture, remembering only how delighted she was always, bless her, with his least success. Imagine, now, if he were going back to lonely digs—or Ruth!

By this time he had reached the crossroads whence the house is visible, and now his bubbling pleasure suddenly went flat. He could see their bedroom windows from here, and there was no light.... He had told her not to sit up, certainly, but he had naturally thought that she would read in bed and keep awake to hear about the evening. Of course he was a little late; but still, he thought resentfully, she might— —

Then he remembered.

How feminine! She wished to spite him for deserting her in favour of the Kit Kats! She was asleep, or anyhow pretending, and thought to punish him, like comic-paper husbands, by making him fumble his way into bed in a considerate darkness!

He smiled at her simplicity. How like her! She knew nothing about anything. He'd soon show her how childish she had been. He meant to turn the light on and bang drawers and then—it really would be rather comic to see her, like the child she was, pretending to awake. In this grim mood of resolution, creditable to a bullied sex, he turned into his gate and as he moved slowly out into the dark garden from under the thick ivy arch, was conscious of a male figure not three feet away.

Instantly his trained imagination nimbly leapt from point to point. He understood now why there was no light up there; he could fancy the poor frightened girl listening to a scraping noise; the useless, snoring servants; possibly a struggle, she was so brave— —

God, if anything had happened to her!

In a second flash he had seen, for the first time possibly, how much she meant to him. We moan our tragedies and scarcely notice blessings till they go.

And whilst his brain sped along those twin paths, his arm sprang out and gripped the fellow by the throat.

"I say, Brett," cried a strangled voice, "it's me."

"Who is it?" asked Hubert. "Alison?" and he released his hold.

"Yes," said the other, making sure that all his throat was there. Brett, he ruefully reflected, was one of those big devils and big devils never knew their strength. "I've been taking your wife to the causerie."

"Oh!" answered Hubert. Perhaps it was excitement only, but he felt of a sudden as though he could resume his grip with pleasure. "It must have been a long affair."

The sneer was obvious. He never had been jealous about Helena before—but things were happening to-night.

"Oh," laughed the other apologetically: and Hubert realised what an ass he was, wondered why he had ever got to know him, "we've been in some time."

"I see," said Hubert. "Well, good-night." He could not trust himself much longer. It was so dark, and that grip had been vaguely satisfying to some primæval side of him....

Geoffrey Alison returned the greeting and slid away with definite relief. He had not liked the way that Brett said that "I see." It was so obvious he did. And then about the causerie having been long— —!

When he grew cooler, sitting in the tube, he began to wonder nervously how this would affect his friendship with Helena (he always thought of her as that), and looked rather doubtfully along the future. Well, he should see. He wouldn't call again until she wrote.

Only one thing was certain. Her husband suspected him—and he felt wickeder than ever....

Hubert meanwhile let himself into the dark hall and merely throwing down his hat, without taking off his coat, strode full of war into the drawing-room. Helena had just finished the postponed yawn with some luxuriance and decided that Mr. Alison must get up very early and do all his work then, and that made him so dull at night. She turned delightedly as the door opened. Good: Hugh already!

"Helena," he said, storming in, "why did you pretend you weren't going to the show to-night?"

"What *do* you mean, Hugh?" she asked, utterly surprised. "I wasn't." She hoped that he had not been drinking. Men, she believed, mostly did when they got out alone.

"You must think me a fool," he said. "But I don't intend to have an argument about it. I only want to say at once that I think it would be far better if you saw less of your friend Mr. Alison. I meant to say it anyhow. People are talking."

"But I don't understand," she faltered, almost as a question.

He laughed scornfully. "I know you're ignorant but you are not a fool, so don't pretend you are. Of course married women don't need chaperons, I know all that, but a mere girl like you and that young ass and almost midnight—but don't let's go into all that." He calmed himself, swallowing his wrath, and said more gently; "I know it's all right really, dear, don't think I don't, it's only—well, you know what people say."

"*What* do they say?" she asked indignantly.

"As you ask," he answered, letting the words out coldly, "I heard one man telling another at the Golf Club yesterday that Mrs. Herbertson was saying she had not yet found out whether Alison or I was Mr. Brett, but thought *he* was as you saw more of him. That's a local joke! It's jolly, isn't it?"

"*I* think it's disgusting," she answered oddly calm. "I shouldn't ever care what people with that sort of mind think."

"Well *I* do," he almost shouted at her, "and I want you to understand as my wife that I forbid you to see that young Alison again. I don't know anything about him except that I did him a favour once. And I don't mean to have it."

"I think you're excited," she said calmly, not at all like the child that he had always known. She gathered new strength from his sudden weakness. One of them must have reserve.

"Excited!" he mocked. "Well, who wouldn't be? A dirty-minded little cad like that!"

"Hubert," she said roused at last, "you've got no right to call him that. It's you and Mrs. Herbertson and every one that have the dirty minds. I don't know what you think. He's not a cad. He's *your* friend and I like him. He's been nice to me." A devil tempted her, urging her on beyond the point of a good friend's defence. "I'm very fond of him," she said, provocatively.

And then that devil entered into Hubert Brett. It had been a full night and excitement all the way. He had not yet recovered from that garden scene. And now, listening to her words, hearing his rival praised, he felt again as he had felt when he thought that some harm had come to her. He seized her in his arms with an unreasoning passion; held her there, resisting; kissed her furiously on lips, eyes, everywhere; laughing and saying: "You are mine, mine. You belong to me, I tell you. You're all mine!"

"Let me go, Hubert," she cried terrified. She could not understand.

He let her go, at that. She moved away and stood behind the table, as though that gave her protection. He gazed at her smiling, panting.

"I'm sorry," he said presently. "It was your fault: you were so maddening. You don't see what it means to me."

The little gods of Comedy laughed out upon the tragic spectacle of a man released by oddly joined emotions from his chains of Self and a wife who wondered in fear whether Kit Kats drank champagne....

"And how did the dinner go off?" she asked soon, in her usual tones.

CHAPTER XIII
SECRETS

Helena came to the conclusion that her mother had been right in one point: life was difficult. She decided further that it was the Mrs. Herbertsons who caused the trouble. Things would be all right if no one ever thought about them!

But she had Consolations beyond this Philosophy.

For one thing, Hubert almost instantly relented, the next day to be precise, about poor Mr. Alison. She, giving way in turn, had said she would appease the vicar's wife and golfers by seeing less of him. So all that stupid fuss was over.

This, however, was not the real Consolation. No, she had a secret.

Helena Brett's secret was not a typically wifely one. It was based, rather, on her childish games. Every little girl has secrets—to the scorn of boys—and when, like Helena, she is an only child, she has them to herself. Of course it is less satisfactory, because although by its nature even a pretending secret needs but one, the whole fun lies in telling it to some one else.

Helena told no one about hers. And it was much more thrilling than those early Devonshire affairs, which largely hinged on the exact position of a fast-decaying mole.

The secret differed too from those of many wives in this, that it was all about a woman; a woman she had never met, a woman she could never meet.

For over a year now, since causeries and lectures on assorted topics began to fit into a shapeless enough whole—a something that explained or might explain what Helena called "Things"—she had put stray thoughts down into a shilling diary. At first they had been merely sentences that touched her or inspired, things heard and read. Then as her mind began to feel its way, she wrote these extracts down, and half ashamed at first, though nobody would ever see them, added her comments on their theories. How elementary the first had been! She blushed, re-reading them. "'The best pilots are ashore'" (ran one on page two). "Then are they really pilots?"

Soon, as was to be expected, she could not endure these accusing words, even herself; and throwing the slim volume pell-mell in the fire, bought and embarked upon a more ambitious tome.

Then indeed began the proper secret, for up till now though nobody had ever known, (she could hear Hubert laughing at her and calling her "so refreshing" ...) it had not been tremendously exciting.

Now it was, however, for the new book, started ambitiously enough as a sort of brief record of her daily moods—she had so much time now that she saw less of Geoffrey Alison—gradually burgeoned into something even more colossal.

They never had been quite her own sensations in this second volume. Those were so extremely dull! No, they had been those of some one like herself: a young wife with a busy husband, some one who felt a fool and wanted not to, wanted very much, but he quite liked it really——oh yes, sometimes, the first day or two, she felt a cad. Hubert really wasn't the least bit like that; it was all over-done; but she supposed that it was easier—he always said it was—if you exaggerated than if you just kept to the truth. It all seemed rather horrid, somehow. She thought about tearing up the book.

And then—just about the time of the Kit Kat affair—began the real, astounding, secret.

Virginia, as she called the wife inwardly (for it was all in the first person)—Virginia began to grow!

It was not Helena's own moods and feelings now that went upon the paper: something endlessly more thorough, more intense, more—well, Helena's own word was "sloppy."

Frankly she despised Virginia. That scene about the Kit Kats came into her diary (it was not Helena's), quite different, about a different thing in fact, and more hysterical. She hoped she would not end up like Virginia! Yet in a way she saw herself there too, just as beneath the husband she could detect ever so cruel a parody of Hubert in his most naughty moments....

But oh, what fun it was!

When Hubert got up nowadays with some remark like; "Well, *I* must do my work!" she no longer felt lonely or out in the cold or inferior or anything. She just said to herself: "And so must I."

It was too splendid, having secrets.

She told nobody; not even Ally, who liked her to be ambitious.

No, it was her secret.

CHAPTER XIV
WAS IT WORTH WHILE?

Love in a cottage is admittedly no failure, quite delightful; but those who have tried it usually end by owning that love in comfort would be no less charming.

So it was with Hubert.

Nobody, he told himself, could be a better little housekeeper than Helena, no little home more fresh and dainty than their own: but though she never worried him, cleverly adapting their ways to a variable income, he was always faced by the uncomfortable thought: "If this book fails—" or "unless I write some short stories—" and after a while these things begin to tell. Within two years from marriage they had told upon Hubert Brett.

And so had come into being that pot-boiler, confessed to Helena with such solemnity on the wide, prudent, spaces of the Heath.

At first he had thought that it would be a hardship to exchange his own realistic method, his studies of character, for those banalities of plot and action independent of all motive, which wearied him even when read, boiled down, in a magazine. But slowly his mood of cynical disdain changed to a real enjoyment, for any task is splendid so soon as a man gets at firm grips with it. He began to see that when once you had got rid of the idea that action must proceed from character, there was a certain joy in letting wild event pile up on wild event and then be rapidly forgotten under even wilder. When once you had abandoned all reserve, there was a fierce delight in splashing pages with unfettered sentiment; making frank puppets think, love, and renounce as they had thought, loved, and renounced since the old fruity days of the three-volume novel. Of course it was all footle, balderdash, but still (he told himself with pride) it was good footle, splendid balderdash. He had bought some of the most "popular" of recent novels in six-penny editions, novels that had brought fortunes to their authors, and by comparison with his, they did the same thing in a bungling manner. No able novelist, he cynically told his wife, had ever tried till now to write a really good bad novel!

Helena loathed the whole enterprise, not only because she vaguely felt that it was marriage with her which had made it needful, but because she thought it so unworthy. And not least unworthy, not least loathsome, did she find his way of talking. It had been so splendid to hear him speak about his work in the old days: and now it was so horrible.

"I've found a title at last," he said, emerging at lunch-time one day when the book was in its revision-stage, and coming to her in the drawing-room as usual.

"Hooray!" she cried, genuinely pleased because he had been worried as to that and this would mean a cheery walk. "What is it? Is it good?"

"Couldn't be better," he replied, and as usual she missed the irony. He paused and then; "*Was It Worth While?*"

"Oh, Hugh," she could not help exclaiming. "That *isn't* the title?"

"Don't you like it?" he enquired sardonically and let himself down cheerily upon the sofa.

Helena of late had begun to express quite elaborate opinions even to Hubert, who somehow always terrified her, rather, when it came to intellect. He was so much cleverer, she knew, and never seemed to take her views as anything except a joke. She always spoke a little timidly. He would have been surprised to hear how cleverly she talked to Alison and others. But that is true of many married couples.

"No," she began slowly. "It's so—I don't know, but—well, so cheap. All your others were so dignified and simple; I think *Wandering Stars* was simply excellent; but this—it sort of reminds me of those plays with names like *Did She Do It?* You know what I mean!"

Hubert smiled grimly. "You seem to think I'm trying to be dignified. Not a bit of it: we're out for money! Money, my dear Helena: no more worry about bills, and our own motor-car!" She could not bring herself to be amused and he went on more moodily: "Do you imagine any woman wants novels with titles that are dignified? and men aren't fools enough to read them. Of course you picked out my best seller for your argument; but look at *The Bread of Idleness*. That was dignified enough and splendidly reviewed and sold two thousand copies; just about a hundred pounds for me for one year's work! No thanks, I've done with dignity, *pro tem*. There may be just about two thousand women with a taste in dignity, but I want all the shop-girls this time: I'm out for my hundred thousand! I want them when they go to the seaside library and pay their twopences to notice *Was It Worth While?*

in big letters on a purple ground. That'll make them think! No more dignity for me: you want to make them think, to make them wonder "Why?" I'd call the book *Why Smith Left Home*, if only it was new."

She did not answer for a few moments: then she said very gently but with a new firmness; "Hugh dear, is it really necessary to do all this? Can't we just go on as we have been doing? I dare say I could manage better, really, and I've often told you I simply don't know what to do with my allowance: it's eating its head off in the bank! Surely we're not so hard up as all that? I hate the whole idea."

"What whole idea?" he asked coldly. One did look for encouragement from one's own wife. He got up to leave her.

"This pot-boiler, as you call it; the title; the way you talk about it; everything. It's all so different, and I've been so proud of the others." She gathered courage and went on: "Look here, Hugh, why not give it up; start on a really good one that'll help your name; and we'll live meanwhile on all that from my allowance in the bank?" She rose and took him by the arm persuasively.

"My dear child," he said with condescension, "you seem to think it's all just money. Tear the whole book up? Don't worry your little head with such things, but just go and see if Lily can't give us some early lunch and then we'll go to Kew for tea!"

Helena, released with a kiss, went out feeling oddly rebellious in spite of the Kew treat; and as for him, he was annoyed. Give it up, indeed! She talked as though "all this" (for she had called it that) were something criminal, instead of merely a book that was bound to sell! He certainly had no idea of sacrificing all his work for her absurd dislikes....

Even the best artists do not so much object to popularity, when they reach thirty-eight.

Hubert Brett, indeed, was more excited over this novel's birth than over that of any other. Almost every day he had to go up to see agent, publisher, or editor. He told Helena, as his excuse for leaving her so much, that it was most important this book, as a "popular" one, should be widely advertised and publishers were such eternal fools about that sort of thing. They always spent all their money upon other people's trash and then said they could not afford to help on your own books!

As the day for publishing drew nearer, this theory bulked almost into an obsession. Helena came to dread the paper boy's arrival. Hubert would tear the dailies open, dash by instinct to the literary page, and then give a discordant laugh of scorn or anger.

"Of course not," he would say. "They won't tell any one till it's been out a week! They mean to keep it dark, trust them!"

"I dare say they're saving up for later on, dear," was her soothing reply. It was not always she, by now, who was the child.

But he would not be soothed.

Helena was glad when the day arrived, although it was a nervous time. He had been full, the night before, of how amusing it would be to hear the critics slang him for a change, instead of finding all those dull superlatives that put the public off: but remembering his past fury with those few reviews which found some blemish in his work, she had her misgivings.

"Only I expect," she said, "it may seem rather curious at first—having bad notices, I mean." She looked across at him covertly and anxiously. She had begun, by now, to knit waistcoats for him and felt as though they had been married for eternity.

Hubert, lounging idly in the other armchair, merely laughed. "Curious? Well, amusing.... It'll certainly be something new to be slated by the critics and rushed after by the libraries. It's usually been the other way about!" He knew, himself, that he would feel the blame from critics who had liked his work, but then— — After all, if the readers liked it and were thousands where they had been hundreds— —! And there was the money....

Next morning the paper boy delivered a specially large roll of papers and Hubert flung himself upon them with unusual vigour. Helena, her eyes fixed on a letter where the words all flickered, was anxious to what might seem an unjustified extent. She could just see him with one corner of her eye.

Paper after paper was torn open; his gaze ran greedily along the columns; but he never paused to read.

At length he flung the last one down with a fierce gesture.

"It's a boycott," he cried petulantly. "I've always had at least two notices, for years, upon the day. We sent them out early on purpose. It's nothing but a boycott."

He seemed to find some consolation in that word with its historical immensity.

"How too bad, dearest," murmured Helena, in duty and with a sinking heart. She saw no cause for any boycott. And she knew that his other novels had better deserved any privilege.

On four dreary mornings the same tragic farce took place, and also with the evening papers. Then on the fifth day Hubert's fast-travelling eyes stopped abruptly, he said "Ha!" and then read out with a naïve joy "*Was It Worth While?*"

"Good," exclaimed Helena, still doubtful.

Suddenly he gave a wild laugh. "I like that," he said. "That is rich." He put the paper down very gently on the table. Then he raised the cover from the buttered eggs.

"What is it, dear?" she compelled herself to ask.

"They say," announced Hubert in extremely level tones, "this habit of publishing a well-known author's early works as new is one that has grown far too common."

Then, letting himself go; "Early works? I'll show them! It is libellous. I can prove my case to the hilt."

"I shouldn't worry with them," she said, feeling inadequate. "Perhaps it will just make the book sell? We expected them to be all nasty, didn't we?" She tried to speak brightly. Then an inspiration came to her. "Perhaps there are some better ones?" she said. The great thing would be to divert his mind. A law-case would be terrible. Nobody got anything, ever, except the barristers.

He passed the heap of unopened papers scornfully across to her. "You look at them," he said. "I don't know why I do or why one cares. They're just a pack of failures. I always despise myself for looking at their stuff at all." He opened a letter with unneeded violence.

With slow unpractised fingers Helena began to search for reviews. "No, no," she said at each, until she thought (he was so quiet), that this might be annoying him and went on with her task in silence.

Then her hands suddenly clutched the paper tightly, symbolic of her effort to say nothing, for her eyes had caught the heading, *Was It Worth While?* The notice ran to half a column and this was an important paper. She blessed her cleverness in having looked.

One moment later, she was blessing her forethought in not saying anything. For this was the review:

"*Was It Worth While?*

"For some time now it has been an interesting question, with those who can find any interest at all in the popular novels of to-day, as to what exactly may be the peculiar touchstone of popularity. We can most of us recall the names of two or three books which have run into their quarter of a million copies, according to advertisements: and in reading them hungrily for a solution of the problem, we have been more than a little astounded by the crudeness of the fare submitted. We have been unwilling, as good optimists of human nature, to believe that mere literary vices can account for any library demand.

"Mr. Hubert Brett, perhaps unconsciously, has done us a good service. We do not, let it be premised at once, refer to our gratitude for his latest novel. Some of Mr. Brett's work, notably *Splendid Misery* and *The Bread of Idleness*, has been praised in these columns for the sincere attempt which the author made in it to get at grips with the problems of real life, forgetting (as few authors can) the fictionists who went before him. In *Was It Worth While?* he seems to have thought, for a change, of almost nothing else. The book is a weird salad of remembered scenes, an olla podrida of episodes we wish we could forget. It would be wasting time and space indeed to attempt synopsis of Mr. Brett's astounding tale—for it is not a novel, however one define that vaguest of all literary products. By lumping together the worst and cheapest portion of all the bad and clap-trap tales which have seen light since printing was unhappily invented, one may arrive at a far better notion of this book than can be gained by wading through its crowded pages. The process, let us add, is also less fatiguing.

"But this is where Mr. Brett has done us, we repeat, a service. *Was It Worth While?* (the name alone is symptomatic) has all the qualities of its successful predecessors: the well-worn types, that call for no brain-effort after work; the utterly untrammelled sentiment; the shapeless slices of religion: he has put into his salad all the right ingredients, except one, which he, less lucky than the other cooks, did not possess. And that ingredient, we now believe, is no less than sincerity. The other writers have done this sort of thing well, because they could do no better; and whilst the large public applauded, we have pitied. Mr. Brett has done this sort of thing, although he can do better; and whilst the public will see through him, we despise his effort. Into his motives it would be impertinent to enquire. Perhaps, after all, the book is a mere literary squib. Mr. Brett, it well may be, has no desire to gull the public into a belief in his weak sentiment and crude religion: he wishes to deride those qualities in others. If so, we congratulate and thank him once again: we understand at last the essential quality (and it is, we confess, a fine one) in the Library big-seller. On any other ground, however, it certainly was not *Worth While*."

Helena did not dare to read all down the column. She read the last words and she bit her lips to keep back tears of which she was ashamed. She knew that it was true—and she hated, loathed the man or woman who had written it. She would give anything, all she possessed, all that poor Hubert had thought he would make from the horrid book, to spare him this review: to shield him from the pain that she knew it was bound to give him.

"Found one?" he asked. Her hands almost dropped the paper.

"No," she said. "There don't seem any more, unless I've managed to miss one. Now I'm seeing what has happened!" And she contrived to laugh.

He appeared to feel relief rather than disappointment.

"You don't often do that," he said cheerily enough. "I thought you despised politics and everything like that?"

"I don't often get the chance to read them," she said and hurriedly turned on to the next page, "considering you always cling firmly to the D.T. till I've got to begin my housework!" This last was her name for what he, in a Yankee spirit, nicknamed "chores."

So for the moment that danger was averted, but Helena knew it was really no more than postponed, and long before the day was over, wished that she had faced it instantly.

When he came in to her just before dinner she knew that he had seen before he spoke a word. He drew the notice, neatly cut out, from his pocket, and she made a pretence of reading it.

"It's merely spite," was all he said. "How dare they call me insincere? They know it's a good seller and that's just what they can't stand. I've written to the editor and I hope I get that swine the boot."

"Is that very kind, dear?" she asked. "It's his job, you know, and you said bad reviews would sell the book."

He gave an angry snort. "Yes, I dare say, but not this kind. No plot, nothing except that its fatiguing and *may* be a burlesque. English people hate being puzzled even more than they hate being bored."

This saying had the effect, she thought, of cheering him a little, for he gave a sardonic laugh and said:

"Well, no matter, let them do their worst. Trust the public later on to find out that the novel's bad! ... When's dinner?"

CHAPTER XV
DISCOVERIES

An Ethical Society might pass a winter's evening in this debate: Does it need more strength to endure failure or to bear success? The dangers upon either road stand out easily, for all but the actual wayfarer. By the one he may fall into the slough of Bitterness, whilst the other, far more pleasant as it draws him on, may lead to no more than the pitiable, luxurious cities of Arrogance and Meanness.

The problem certainly needs no elaboration in this place, since Hubert's path lay all too clearly towards failure. "I fear," wrote his publisher as an old friend, "it is no use concealing the fact that people do not want the book. There have as yet been no repeat orders from libraries or booksellers. We can only face the fact and hope to do better with the next. As you know, in my opinion the book was not up to your usual high level."

"Who wants his damned opinion?" growled Hubert out loud, though alone, and crumpled up the letter. Why, publishers weren't even critics!

As to these last, their unanimity for once was wonderful.

There are ingenious authors who amuse themselves by printing excerpts from reviews of their last novel, alternately conflicting, thuswise; "An able novel: *Tooting Sentinel*. Weak and formless: *Times*. An arresting piece of work, whoever by: *Stafford News*. An amateur affair: *Standard*;"—thinking in this manner to have blackened for evermore the ancient art of Criticism in any decent-minded person's eyes. They scarcely realise, poor injured souls, that the thing is an Art. Were it but a machine, it doubtless would attain the same result from each book, whether put before it by a Fleet Street expert or a Stafford tyro. Because it is an Art, however, and all Art is merely the expression of an individual emotion, it follows that each book must react on every critic in a different way. These notices, so pompous with *The Times* or *Stafford News* above them, are not worked out with prayer by the whole paper's staff; they stand for one opinion, no less—and no more—than the opinion of a woman-reader over the tea-tray. Opinions, moreover, vary; praise to God! How fresh and hopeful, what a message, seems this story to the un-read Staffordian; how stale and hopeless, what an ancient dish, it appears to him of Printing House Square, who has read more than he can hope ever to forget!

And yet beneath it all there is a principle. Bad Of Its Sort is bad, whatever sort one likes; which is all Plato's Ideas in a convenient nutshell.

And every one agreed that *Was it Worth While?* was bad of its sort. It tried to be something it was not, and what can be more shocking?

Hubert, then, had an admirable chance of showing what effect a failure, after some years of moderate success, had on his character; and took it to the full. As the reviews came in, he grew more and more violent. It was not many days before he countermanded all the extra papers, but his faithful Press-Cutters sent in the notices religiously and he could not help reading them. Helena would come down first (she always did) at breakfast time and hide the small green envelopes, which then arrived by the last post and were brought in at 9 p.m. by the complaisant Lily.

Then what a flow of words! Poor critics, publishers, and readers; what a set they were, how blind, how asinine, how spiteful! Sometimes he would at once go to his study and write a reply, which Helena did not in every case succeed in rescuing before it got into the pillar-box, though certainly her score was bigger.

It was a trying month and he did not spare even her. When there were no reviews to tear verbally—and sometimes other ways—in fragments, he would moan plaintively that this meant he would never get another sou out of the book beyond the small advance already paid, and nobody would want to read the next one either, and Heaven knew how they would pay the house-bills.

"I don't suppose any one will even publish it," he would say, almost gloating, like a schoolboy probing his cut finger.

"Oh, Hugh!" she cried, believing him, "it does seem awful. And to think you were so successful till you married me and had to write this terrible pot-boiler. Oh, how I wish you'd never done it!"

"What, married you?" he asked, suddenly laughing. "Bother shop! Come along out and see if we can't find a good stick to throw for the hound;" and as he passed, he kissed her on the hair and drew her up on to her feet.

His moods were so abrupt, just now, that sometimes she grew frightened.

It was lucky, then, that she had got her consolation; the great secret. Geoffrey Alison was far less frequent in the house these days, not having totally forgotten yet that grip upon his throat, and she would have been very desolate when Hubert was locked in with his work if she could not have flown excitedly to hers. Absorbed entirely in the opinion and career of the increasingly contemptible Virginia, she found herself free for a while from all the worries of real life, returning to them with a mind refreshed as by the most luxurious of sleep; the reason why there will be always writers, even when cinemas and cheap editions have made it not a paid, but an extravagant, profession.

So utterly absorbed was she, indeed, about six weeks after the fatal day of publication, that the drawing-room door was open before she had noticed any warning noise outside. Helena realised that it was far too late by now to hide the sheets of manuscript and substitute a letter, as she always did. Any attempt like that would only make detection certain—and far worse.

To her relief it was not Hubert, only Mr. Alison, with Lily holding the door open. She would not so much mind his knowing—he was so encouraging—supposing that he noticed.

And this of course he promptly did.

"Hullo!" was in fact his very first remark. "Are you too among the authors?" He waved his hand towards the little pile of manuscript that should have been inside a drawer.

"Yes," she said, hoping that she was not blushing. "But not too loud as it's an awful secret. Hubert doesn't know."

He tip-toed at it with exaggerated caution. "Oh-ho!" he whispered. "Then I guess: it's all about him! It is a safety-valve."

This was a little joke: they were devoted, he knew, though he could never understand what she saw in the great, conceited, selfish brute: but Helena felt sure now that the blush was there.

"No," she was bound to answer, and when he asked, "Fiction?" in surprise, it must be "Yes." And so it was, by now, she argued. A safety-valve at first perhaps, because Hugh seemed to loathe her having even the most usual ideas, but fiction certainly by now, for the ideas of Virginia were not her own ideas; the silly, sloppy thing!

"I'm going to read it please," he said and began collecting the loose pages (the book had long ago been cast aside).

"Certainly not," she answered, very dignified, and trying to forget that they were the words of a comic song she had heard on the gramophone.

"Oh, but yes," he answered.

"Give it to me," she said, turning now to melodrama for her catch-phrase.

He held the prize by sitting on it. "Listen," he began, as staidly argumentative as though he had been drunk: and then he paused. "If you let me read it," he said presently, "I'll tell you what I think of it and I bet it's original. If you don't let me read it, I shall tell—your husband!"

"You wouldn't be such a cad," she answered. She never knew when he was serious, because he often looked most funny then.

"I'm not so sure," he said. "Anyhow let me? I'll begin to-night."

"You won't do that," she retorted laughingly, "because the first bit's in a volume, locked away upstairs."

He whistled. "What! An opus? Tut! Now don't be selfish. When you first wanted to know about Art, I told you all I could, and now you're doing things, I think it's only fair that I should be the first to see."

He looked so funny, leaning forward eagerly yet taking care to keep his weight still on the manuscript, that she laughed heartily. He surely wasn't serious now?

He looked extremely hurt. "Very well," he said, getting up. "If you think it's so funny, that's all right. I suppose, now, you've done with me: you've got all out of me you needed: so now you don't even tell me that you're trying to create." He got up from the bureau with much dignity and moved towards the door. One sheet of the manuscript stuck to his clothes until he reached the centre-table. She was just wondering what to do about this, when it fluttered downward. That broke her inaction.

"Oh, no," she said, "don't be stuffy. I never meant it. I thought you were being ironical about my 'art' and I can't ever see it. Please don't be offended, Ally." In spite of her announced resolve she hardly ever called him that, and now she said it with a slight burr, dwelling on it till the name became a thing of beauty, almost a caress.

He wavered at the door; but he was shrewd in business by heredity. "Well, will you let me read it?" he said firmly.

"Yes, if you really want to," she replied. "I'll fetch the other half." Secretly she longed for an opinion, and she would never dare to ask for Hubert's. "Promise not to look at this bit," she said, coy as a young singer. "I couldn't bear you to see it till you are right away."

He promised and she left him to his thoughts, which were of an expectant nature. She was a girl that he had never really understood (in actual practice he had very small experience of girls), and he knew well enough that first books, even when all fiction, are half true. He was amused inwardly at her simplicity in lending him the manuscript.

She came back with something like a baby scrap-book in her hand. "I got bored with writing in this," she said. "It was so uncomfortable, the edges cut my hand." Then, as though half repenting; "You must promise not to look at it till you get home and never to tell Hubert."

"Is that likely?" he asked, referring to the last condition. It made the business far more thrilling.

He had the common sense, however, to see that she was already doubtful of her wisdom: so that as soon as volume and loose sheets were in his hand, he changed the subject tactfully.

"Well," he asked, "and how is the new book going?"

"Oh, isn't it awful?" Helena replied. "I don't know if I ought to tell you, but it's not sold at all: not, I mean, except those sold before publication and I never understand quite how that happens."

"Then I expect it's good," said Geoffrey Alison a trifle cheaply.

Helena replied with emphasis, as though rebutting a grave charge. "*No*, not at all. That's just it: it's much worse than his other ones. He's in an awful way. I don't believe he's sold a thousand copies!"

"My dear Mrs. Brett," he said (he always hated calling her that, but he dared not embark on "Helena"), "comfort yourself with the idea that a thousand copies is a very good sale for any decent novel. Each copy, after all, is read by twenty people in these days of libraries, so that means twenty thousand readers. Of course if Hubert wrote for shop-girls, he might find a million: but do you think that any really serious study of real life—the sort of book that simply gets at character and doesn't fuss with plot: the real, artistic novel—is going to find more than twenty thousand people in dull old England who can understand it? And that's your thousand-copy sale! I don't mind betting no really 'artistic' novel—it's a beastly word—ever sells more than that."

His one idea in all this had been to console her, for he guessed a little what it meant when Hubert Brett was "in an awful way"; but now she seemed if anything more troubled. She sat in dazed silence, looking like a small child who has seen something which it absolutely cannot understand at all.

"But *Wandering Stars*," she said presently, "I've often heard, sold quite five thousand."

"Oh yes, I dare say," came the unthinking answer. Had she forgotten about her MS.?

"Well, wasn't that artistic?" There was a note of battle in her voice.

He saw now where he had drifted. "Oh yes," he began. "But not quite in the way I meant. That was a good story, very, and was popular. I meant, really, quite a different sort of book." He floundered in excuses.

"What sort?" she asked pitilessly. "Better ones?"

"Oh no," he said, more and more embarrassed. "Not that exactly. You can't say that. You can't compare different kinds in Art. You've got to judge a man by his success in what he has attempted. A good caricature is much better than a bad Madonna," and firmly upon Art with the feeling of a mariner safe in port after a storm, he drew her mind away—or so he thought, this man who knew so little about women—and after a while, sooner than usual, made his excuses and departed.

Outside he got as near to saying "Whew!" as any live man ever has. He had jolly nearly put his foot in it! He wouldn't for millions let that little girl suspect that really artistic people—his own set—did not think so much of Brett's work as Brett did himself. What a lumbering idiot he had been! The fact was, he had thought she meant to get that writing of hers back and he had wanted to distract her mind. In that, anyhow, he had succeeded.

On the way back, he could not resist dipping into the book as he walked.

He skimmed a page and chuckled Fiction? He recognised himself already!

CHAPTER XVI
A MATTER OF SALES

Long after Geoffrey Alison had gone, Helena sat motionless at her desk, biting a pen-holder; looking out into the garden and thinking.

She was not thinking, as he would have imagined, about her manuscript. She was thinking about Hubert's work.

In one sense she had no great opinion of Geoffrey Alison, although she liked to have him as her friend. She did not respect him, did not think him manly, would never be swayed by his estimate of her: he was an odd, amusing, clever, little thing and she was never altogether sure when he was serious. But in another way she thought more of his words than even she had ever admitted to herself. Hubert had never taken her development as serious at all; had made it clear he thought her stupid, as he said once, "to burden her dear little head with brains, when she was so original already"; so that it had been Mr. Alison (who must be really very kind, at any rate) that had initiated her into the thrilling mysteries of Art. He had taken her round galleries, to lectures; told her this was bad or that good, then tried to show her why; and though they argued nowadays, her basic views were his: she judged things by the touchstone he had given her. What then more natural than that she should value his ideas on Art?

And now—now he had told her (oh, without meaning it, she knew, but that made it no better)—told her that Hubert's novels were not thought artistic really, they were good stories but no more, and not in the same class as vague others which sold always badly. She had been so proud of them, until *Was It Worth While?* appeared; and now it seemed that all the others had belonged to a class of no merit, too. They were good of their sort—like a caricature...! Hubert had always spoken with such scorn of novels which were "popular": and now she had heard Mr. Alison joining that fatal adjective to his pet *Wandering Stars*....

It may be thought peculiar that Helena should have believed so easily; but as she sat there and gazed out through unseeing eyes, nothing of any weight stood in the other balance.

When she had married him, proud of his name, she was a simple girl. She had not read a word of his until she was engaged: and how could she judge after that, if she had been the best of critics? Then, once his wife—well, who would tell her anyhow? Ally, she knew, had never meant to and she liked him better than she had, for it. Hubert was so contemptuous about his paintings, that she knew he must have often felt the obvious temptation to revenge.

Hubert, in fact, had been so scornful about everybody else's work. In Literature—she now recalled—she had relied entirely on his estimates. Mr. Alison, till now, had said he really was no judge of books and told her she must ask her husband.... She had got the idea that Hubert's work was of the best sort, the most properly artistic, and when she wondered why it did not make more money, he had said that it was too good....

Now with a shock that somehow loosened far more than merely her ideas on books, this young wife learnt that the great Hubert Brett, with all his endless moods—the house revolving round his inspiration—only created novels which were "popular" in class, yet nearly always failed to sell!

She had not of course got the matter quite so definite as that in her own mind, when there came to her ears the warning sound of his door opening. There were no sheets of manuscript to hide to-day, but she put down a cedar pen-holder which had grown very ragged at the top in a half-hour.

"Well," she said, leaping up and forcing herself, like a trained wife, to be cheery, "what success to-day?" She always asked him that. He liked it.

Hubert was not satisfied to-day. "Rotten," he said; "absolutely rotten. That idiot Lily had put all the candle-sticks and things the wrong way round on my writing-desk and I'd to move them all, just when I got there feeling in the mood to work."

"Oh, I'm so sorry, dear," she answered humbly. "I will tell her." She knew, you see, the whole of a wife's duty now.

"Don't worry about that, my dear," he said without much conviction; "but these housemaids seem to think an artist is a sort of navvy who only wants a pen and everything's all right. They don't understand that when you're doing work like mine, the least thing out of its accustomed place catches your eye and absolutely breaks the inspiration: you get up to move it. I never worked back to the proper state at all this morning. I might as well have played a round of golf."

Helena, with a curious sensation that was almost fear—fear, it may be, of herself—realised that his plaint, oft-heard, left her cold this morning. Till now she had always thought how wonderful he was, how different from her dull self, how sensitively made. To-day she felt—she felt that it was all a needless fuss! This last half-hour had crystallised thoughts vaguely growing during a whole year.

She could not trust herself to any comment. She felt that probably all writers had these affectations, and yet there *was* this sudden lack of sympathy about the candlesticks....

"But I hope," she merely said, "the new book's working out all right?"

Hubert dropped upon the sofa, a dead weight of hopelessness. "I don't believe," he said, "I'm meant for an author—not in these days anyhow, when it's a trade. You know, my dear, it's too absurd but I can *not* forget those beastly critics! They've put me off entirely. Every line I write, I think that such and such a paper won't like that: just as though I was writing for them and not for the public!" He took up a magazine and flung it down violently on the sofa. "I tell you though," he said confidently, as though that changed his mood, and rose to go: "I jolly well mean to get at the public, *this* time."

"Hugh," she said, ludicrously horror-struck, "it's not another pot-boiler?" She had not dared to ask and he had vouchsafed literally nothing yet.

He smiled grimly, standing by the door. "You'll see," he said. "I'm nearly through with the synopsis now and I'll read you the first chapter soon. It's not like the last, anyhow. It's called *Eternity*. And there's one thing," he went on with a kind of brutal joy, "if it's a frost, we shall absolutely have to pack up and move off into cheaper quarters: I can't afford to keep you here!"

"But, Hugh," she began in sympathetic protest.

But he had closed the door, outside.

CHAPTER XVII
THE TEMPTER

Helena did not possess the vice of introspection.

Conscious as she was that something had changed in her attitude towards her husband's moods and work, those tyrants of her married life to which till now she had bowed down so humbly, she told herself in a general way that things would soon shake down again, that it was probably her fault, and that she must make sure what Mr. Alison had really meant. This time she would keep him to it and not let him drift off to Madonnas. She wished he would make haste and call. Why had she lent him all that stuff about Virginia? He was probably wondering what on earth to say to her about it and that was why he did not call. What a nuisance he was! She longed to ask him definitely what people really thought of Hubert's work and whether he had meant all that. You never really knew, with him....

When, however, he finally arrived, it was with such an air of mysterious excitement that she was forced to wait a moment.

He stood in silence until Lily's heavy steps had died away and then, in a stage whisper: "Is Hubert safely out of hearing?"

"Yes," she laughed. He always amused her when he was funny like this. "He always works, you know quite well, from five till seven. I suppose all this 'sshing is because you want to give me back my silly manuscript. Where is it?" She was glad, in a way, that he was going to be stupid over it.

"Ah," he replied, "that's it," and raised a cryptic finger.

"You *are* funny," she said lazily from her armchair, like some one who claps in the stalls.

He looked slightly hurt. "You always say that if I'm serious," he protested. Then less plaintively, as though heartened by what was to come: "As a matter of fact though, I've done you a very good turn."

"Me?" asked Helena, as he made an effective pause and there seemed nothing else to say. She couldn't thank, in case it really was a joke.

"Yes, you. Your silly manuscript, as you like to call it, is good—jolly good. I don't suppose you realise that, do you? It's something original, these days, and that is everything. It's——"

"I'm glad it amused you," Helena said, thinking that he had quitted himself well and now she must help him out; "but——"

"But where's the good turn?" he broke in, interpreting her wrongly. "Well, I'll tell you. I showed it—I knew you wouldn't mind——" (and here he looked a little timidly at her sideways), "I showed it to a publisher I've met about, a very decent fellow——"

"How dare you?" Helena flashed out youthfully, just as though they were playing Interruptions. "I lent it you to read and I think——"

He kept up the game. "Listen," he said with a firmness rare in him, confident of what he had to tell. "He said it was new and vital and had money in it: those are his exact words; and he wants to publish it if you can think of a good ending. There!"

At last it was out and he stood complacent, waiting for her thanks: but she was not even appeased. "I don't care *what* he said," she cried, and for this moment of her childish anger it was true. "I only know I lent it you and not to him; do you think I want everybody reading all my diaries?"

"But it was not a diary," he answered, keeping his head clear, "and he had no idea of course who wrote it."

"He would, though, if he published it." She thought that she had crushed him; but he merely gained fresh hope, seeing her dally thus with the idea.

"Never," he replied dramatically. "Nobody will ever know except yourself and me."

Before that masterly touch, "will," she crumpled up, and fell back on a new line of defence. "I can't believe," she said, more peaceable, "he's serious. I know quite well, and so do you, it's nothing: just to make the time go while I was alone. I took no trouble: wrote it any odd old time."

"You surely don't imagine," he said, "writers really have to wait for times and seasons and the proper mood? They could work ten to six like anybody else, except it wouldn't be artistic. Do you imagine nothing's good unless it's written with a lobelia in front of you and all that sort of thing? Some of the world's best stuff has come out of an attic. The whole thing's nothing but a pose."

She had her answer about Hubert, without asking. Geoffrey Alison, two years discreet, had suddenly begun to throw bricks in this happy home, and never even heard the crash.

"Oh," she said, lingering on the syllable till it grew into three.

He did not understand. He saw her hesitate and he threw all his weight to drive her the way he desired. "After all," he said, using that most persuasive of openings to a temptation or a fallacy, "what right have you, artistically, to keep to yourself a thing that may please and help millions? You especially, who don't even approve of private Art Galleries because you can't see them! ... I know what it is, exactly; you're thinking of your husband, naturally; but he need never know. I'll do the business, all of it, and show you any notices and no one else will ever guess at all. Think what fun it would be!" (He saw her eyes light up and knew that he had won.) "Besides there'll be the money too and any one can do with that."

"Yes," said Helena, clinging to an earlier sentence, as women will, "but the manuscript gives it away hopelessly that I'm an author's wife, on almost every page."

"Well, how many authors do you think there are?" he said; then with the Tempter's fluency, "and they notoriously marry more than any one. Who in the world could guess? Every one would think that it was by a man. They always do if anybody writes a very intimate peep at a woman's soul." He smiled, remembering how intimate the peep in question sometimes was. "Fancy reading all their silly guesses! Come on! You can't be so selfish!"

Her eyes glistened and she moved on to an earlier point. "It wouldn't really bring much money, would it?" she asked. "Books don't seem to, ever."

"Blatchley—that's the publisher—thinks it would sell like anything: he says it's new. That's why he wants it. There isn't any sentiment in Blatchley. He's right, too: people love these human documents. I dare say it'd bring in several hundred pounds."

Helena gasped. He had offered her the proper fruit at last, this worried little child of Eve, who, feigning to cut down the household bills, had long time satisfied a husband intolerant of change by drawing on her bank account, now perilously near its end.

"What should I call myself?" she answered simply. Several hundred pounds—and all the fun as well!

He thought a moment. "Not Helena," he said with firmness. "They'd guess. Besides no authoress could ever be called Helena: it sounds like Eleanor after a careless housemaid's accident."

"Joan is my second name," she answered humbly.

"Joan," he repeated, and she felt quite ashamed already: he made it sound so long and flat. "No, no; not Joan. That is like Jones with the last letter dropped. It must be something literary. I know." He hesitated, as though weighing the discovered nugget: then, satisfied; "We'll call you Zoë Baskerville."

"Splendid!" she laughed. Already this was a new interest in life. Then a doubt struck her. "*Are* those literary names? Who were they both?"

"I'm blest if I know," he confessed; "but I've seen both in catalogues." So that was settled.

"I never liked Helena for you," he said. "Zoë is just the name. I shall always think of you as Zoë." Then, greatly daring, with a swift rush; "May I call you Zoë?"

He felt as though he were upon the absolute edge of his chair, but she seemed to think nothing of his question. "If you like it," she said, off-hand. "You want some revenge for Ally! But not in front of Hugh or he'll guess when the book comes out, and that would be too terrible."

"No," he said with feeling, "that shall be our secret," and leant slightly forward.

"When will it appear?" she asked excitedly: and he was as near cursing the book, now, as he had been to blessing it, a moment earlier.

He left the house, however, shortly before seven o'clock, stepping upon air. He had never expected to get her consent. Old Blatchley would think him no end of a clever devil and Blatchley was a useful man. Besides, the comedy and excitement of it all! And, best of all, it was a new bond with—Zoë!

Gad, fancy having a ripping little girl like that as pal; and a secret between them absolutely, from her husband even; and calling her Zoë, which he knew in some odd Greek way was a jolly daring sort of name, though he forgot quite how....

Yes, Geoffrey Alison was satisfied.

And as for Helena, with certain shapeless misgivings and fears there mingled a most natural exaltation: since whether one writes for fame or mere "fun," what can be more exciting than the acceptance of one's first book by the first publisher who sees it?

She still could not understand it. She did not realise of course how fresh her view of married life had been: she did not guess perhaps in quite what sense her new-appointed agent had used the word "intimate"; she did not realise that the book's very blemishes were its chief claim to Truth. She could see nothing in the thing at all.

But it was all exciting, very. She would just end it up: make poor Virginia, who was Zoë now, work her way round to happiness, as Ally had said that she must not kill her; then send it up to him and he had vowed she should not even get a single letter; he literally would "do the rest." Then if it failed, no harm was done and she had made her secret yet more thrilling: whilst if in some mad way the book caught on and she received those hundreds—well what a blessing they would be just now with bills, and Hubert who was so silly with practical affairs like that would merely imagine that she was running things more cheaply. (Every woman, deep down, thinks every man a child.)

Besides—if Geoffrey Alison stepped lightly homewards upon air, Helena too felt that the grey world stretched a little softer under her. That shapeless longing for development of a real Self, that almost morbid shame of her own ignorance, had issued finally in something tangible. She was an authoress!

No doubt her book was not like Hubert's, built up carefully on scientific scaffolding; but still—it had pleased Mr. Alison and it had satisfied a publisher!

Small wonder, then, if totally forgetful though she was of her new theories on Hubert's mode of work—immersed by now in the palpitating thrill of her new secret—she yet sat opposite to him this night at dinner with a less feeling of abasement, a new confidence. She found it hard at moments to attend to him and throw in, as she usually did, appreciative comments now and then.

"Of course," he was saying now, criticising a review, "all this about 'painting' with a pen is rubbish. The two arts have no resemblance. The painter used to be a monk—and is a mountebank! He never yet has been a writer."

"Oh, I don't know. What about Rossetti? Or even Whistler?" she put in absently, just as though it had been Geoffrey Alison.

Hubert was brought up with a jerk. He hated people who corrected one. It was like Mrs. Boyd, exactly. Of course he knew that she was right and he wrong, handsomely—although he'd no idea *she* knew—but it would be so dull if every one was accurate!

"My dear," he said coldly, "I know all about that, but do you think you need interrupt my argument to tell me? I shall be afraid to speak at all if I am going to be heckled!"

He waved the thing aside with a short laugh, as though to say she was forgiven. But something in his manner had annoyed Helena to-night.

"I wasn't 'heckling'," she said, trying to speak lightly; "but you know, Hugh, it's a bit mediæval if I know things and mayn't say anything!"

Hubert gaped at her.

Mediæval! That was a real Mrs. Boyd idea. He made no answer, but he was more than vaguely annoyed. This was his simple little Helena no longer. It was those damned lectures....

He felt that from this moment they stood on a new footing.

PART III
HELENA BRETT'S CAREER

CHAPTER XVIII
ZOË

Helena unfolded the slip, pasted on its blue half-sheet, and began to read it, thoroughly engrossed. She seemed forgetful of Geoffrey Alison, who in turn watched her with hardly less attention, more anxiety. He knew the thing by heart.

"*Confessions of an Author's Wife* (Blatchley & Co.) is by its name confessed as of the Human Document category, and this sort of book is never without its attraction. The present volume, chastely bound in green appropriately virginal, recounts the growth of a young girl married to a more or less successful author. Zoë Baskerville, who on one page lets somebody call her Virginia (a lapse not making for conviction), tells in the first person her laudable efforts to develop an ego in the face of a husband who has enough of it for ten. His selfish absorption in his own moods and the conditions suitable to his own labours not unnaturally create in Zoë a feeling of thwarted ambition, which results in a watered, girlish, form of cynicism about Man and Woman. This, however, passes off in the last chapter, where for some reason not easy of access to the mere reader Zoë suddenly sloughs her despondency and bursts into an exultant Credo: 'I believe that Life, all in all, is the most splendid gift a kind God could give to his children. I believe that Man'—and so on for the last four pages.

"It will be seen that subtlety and cohesion are not the strongest points in these confessions, which we hope we have taken seriously enough. About their popularity there can be no doubt. The book possesses pathos, humour, freshness; a mixture beyond failing; and moreover, impinges on life, married life, at moments with a frankness more essentially French than English. This fact may induce those still in Zoë's earlier mood of cynicism to suspicion a male, Fleet Street, author: but for our part, remembering the naïveté of female Youth and that incriminating name Virginia, we are quite ready to accept the volume's authenticity, if we misdoubt somewhat The End's sincerity.

"Taken thus, as a real document, the book has a persuasive charm. Pathetic little Zoë is a figure as real as her selfish husband, who emerges in some way as less great than has been actually stated. (Perhaps we were wrong in denying the book any subtlety.) We can foresee a long and lucrative discussion as to the Author's identity. For our part, we make a gift of the discovered clue 'Virginia,' and shall wait patiently until the publisher, as a good man and true, duly announces the authorship before issuing a cheap edition. Till that day we shall hope to live our lives in much the same round as before."

Helena stared so long at the narrow slip, obviously deep in thought, that Geoffrey Alison found his anxiety turn to a nervous guilt.

Of course, he told himself, he knew the part that worried her in this, her first review. He would have kept it back if he had been quite sure that she would never see it. He rather wished now that he had. It was that stupid bit of course about more French than English. He only hoped they wouldn't all be like that—and none of them worse.

He recalled, as moment joined past moment, his own amusement at some of the passages. They had solved all his problems about Helena. No one but a really innocent girl could be so frank, because to the impure all truth is suspicious. It was only after reading these delicious passages two or three times that Geoffrey Alison, getting a tardy view of the whole book, realised how it might interest the world at large and seem worth while to that shrewd devil Blatchley.

Now, when still she sat impassive, looking at that notice with a slight frown on her forehead, he began to suspect that possibly he had been just a little of a cad. He ought perhaps to have warned her that some of it, though absolutely all right if everybody had pure minds, — —

Yet after all, how could he have told her that? It would be jolly awkward, you know, and only putting ideas into her head. Besides, of course, with those bits cut out, Blatchley would probably have called it tame and struck.... His silence had been really for her good.

At last these alternate surges of guilt and self-justification grated on his nerves. He could endure her silence not a moment longer.

"That's only the first one," he said; "and it's not much of a paper." Now for the reproaches! Better to turn the tap on than to shiver, waiting.

But not for the first time he had misjudged her. It was not that part of the review which had struck home to her so different mind.

"Do you really think the husband stands out as such a brute as all that?" she surprised him by asking.

"No. I thought it exactly like Hubert," was his answer. He could not read her mind; he said the first thing that came into his.

He could not have said a worse. It strengthened all her doubts, fears, and regrets. She really had forgotten, almost, what was in the book. It had been written in such hot excitement and she had scarcely read it since. Ally would not let her see the proofs; he said it wasn't safe, with Hubert there.... She had imagined that the wife was far more silly than herself, the husband altogether different from Hubert. Now, reading that synopsis, she saw (for the first time), how truly that summed up their married life: she *had* wished to "develop an ego," he *had* thwarted her. He would read it too, that or another, and suspect. Then he would get the book—and know. And he would think she meant it all, meant all the wild complaints of Zoë, Zoë whom at first she used to think of as "sloppy" Virginia!

It was too horrible. She loathed the stupid book, she wished that she had never shown it. She loathed Geoffrey Alison. If poor old Hubert ever saw...!

"I suppose we can't possibly suppress the book?" she jerked out suddenly.

Her conversation was more startling than ever to the male brain, to-day. "Suppress it on the strength of the first notice? When it's been out two days? And when the notice says there can't be any doubt about its popularity? Suppress it, indeed! What about friend Blatchley?"

Helena gave a little sigh of absolute despair. It had been so exciting until now: the little green book, locked away upstairs, and libraries actually buying it before it was out, just in the weird way they did Hubert's and real people's!

Now she loathed the book and feared it.

There was terror indeed in her very tones. "But you don't think," she said, "they really can ever find out who the writer was? They seem to think it's only a question of time. Mr. Blatchley couldn't be so mean."

"My dear Zoë" (he felt bound to soothe her and it was so thrilling to say), "how can they possibly? There isn't any 'they' about it. I'm the only person in the world who knows and I suppose you can trust *me?*" He got up from the sofa whilst speaking and struck an attitude quite close to her, at the last words.

"Of course I do, Ally; you're a splendid pal and I know you will never breathe a word. It means a lot to me you see;" and she just pressed his hand.

It was not much perhaps, but it meant a great deal to him. *He* did not loathe the book.

CHAPTER XIX
BUSINESS

Helena's oppression, as of some impending blow, refused to disappear. She could not believe, whatever Geoffrey Alison might say, that their secret could be kept until the end. Every fresh notice of the book caused fresh alarm. With one accord reviewers harped upon the authorship, some of the less reputed papers embarking upon guesses.

That, to Mr. Blatchley's genuine delight, began denials. He eagerly collected all of them, and not a month had passed before Geoffrey Alison arrived full of importance and excitement. He came, now, almost daily after five; as often, quite, as in the old days before the garden-scene with Hubert; his mind full of the need to cheer this poor sad Zoë who got no joy at all from her success. Surely as it grew and there was still no prospect of detection, she would begin to think of all the money she was earning and enjoy the praise? He hoped so.

"Look at this," he said keenly, waving an extract at her.

Her tones were dull. "What is it? Another review?"

"No, an advertisement. Awfully clever and suits our game too!"

He held it out to her. In bold print it ran thus:

"WHO?

"Already the wives of the following famous authors have publicly declared that they did NOT write

CONFESSIONS OF AN AUTHOR'S WIFE."

(Here followed a list of eight names.)

"Ah! But who did?

WHO?"

"I don't see it suits us at all," she said without enthusiasm.

"Why, it's putting people on the wrong track," he tried to argue.

She would not have it. "It's making people want to know when they don't really care a bit," she said with a ripe worldly wisdom quite beyond her years.

And soon, to Mr. Blatchley's yet greater delight, people did begin to care. They cared so much, in fact, that they all read the book in order to find out. And nobody knew even then. It was, however, something to discuss at boring dinner-parties; so every one was pleased. Every one but Helena.

Reading the book afresh, she was astounded, terrified, to see how near it was to life. She had thought it all altered beyond recognition: fiction merely based on fact. But now she realised that all the parts of it which mattered—Zoë's ambitions, her husband's repression—were true, truer than she ever knew indeed: whilst all the variations—names, place, ages, children, work—made no real difference at all. In all life it is the soul alone that matters, for there lies happiness and all those others are mere accidents. And the soul of Zoë was the soul of Helena; the life of Helena, the life of Zoë. Reading her book, she realised for the first time her life.

Daily the thing became more of a nightmare.

Hubert, of course, noticed nothing: but Geoffrey Alison grew weary of her constant admonitions as to silence.

"Oh, for Heaven's sake, Zoë," he cried at last (for he was getting almost husbandly in his remarks, encouraged by their common secret), "do try and get rid of the idea that 'all is discovered' and I'm a silly ass or else a beastly cad!"

"It isn't that," she answered with a gloomy petulance; "but something might easily happen and I simply don't know how I should face Hubert."

"Hubert? Why, I expect he would be jolly proud of you."

"Proud?" she repeated bitterly; "when he has been so splendid to me always, and here I am making him out a selfish brute who sacrifices his wife's happiness to his career and me a poor little bullied creature who goes upstairs and cries. He'd never believe that it was all exaggerated—and nor, of course, would anybody else. Proud, indeed? I do like that!"

Indeed, when she thought of what an awful thing she had done, Helena very often could have gone upstairs like flabby Zoë (née Virginia) and wept.

Geoffrey Alison at length got thoroughly impatient with her.

He was enjoying it all hugely and he failed to see why she should not enjoy it too. Every day he opened his paper eagerly to see what new scheme the resourceful Blatchley had devised to spur a public interest which as yet showed no signs of flagging.

Helena, in sympathy with her whole scheme, had much exaggerated the eminence of the Husband's position. It was not a case of any back-street Kit Kats here: he was away, night after night, delivering most brilliant lectures to exclusive West End literary clubs or even travelling four hundred miles to unveil well-earned lapidary tributes of great authors who had actually managed to be dead now for a hundred years. This husband, who deserted his wife and was jealous if she went to anything with any other man, was not an author of the Hubert Brett class, so that big names were thrown about at parties where in very truth the problem soon became a topic. Each had it on the best authority that So-and-So, the celebrated author, or Mrs. So-and-So, had said this or the opposite; and nobody believed the other's story.

Nothing sells a book like talk. The printed word, paid or unpaid, is only useful to set tongues a-wagging. And as the authorship was bandied here and there, editions trickled slowly from the Press.

Mr. Blatchley was delighted. His firm was not among the old-established, and this could rank as his first great success; but it was very great. The book was only three-and-six; people actually bought it; the libraries roared out for more.

Journalists, hot upon dinner-table topics as vultures after flesh, interviewed him, each hoping to be in the office at that crucial moment when he decided the book's sale would gain by an announcement of the much-debated name.

But even when the interest began to wane—for nothing lasts Londoners more than a fortnight—Mr. Blatchley to every one's surprise was adamant. He still persisted in the stupid lie that he had not found out, himself....

"Look here, Alison," he said one day, when Geoffrey Alison had called in at his little office off the Strand, "you're not playing cricket, quite." He was a podgy little alien man, fattened beyond his years, and he said this with all a British sportsman's sternness.

"Oh come, you know; don't say that," exclaimed the other, naturally shocked. (His life average in the game itself would be a decimal.)

"I do, though," said the publisher and offered him a cigar. The artist did not care for that especial form of smoke, but felt that this was not the moment to be firm. He must not lose further prestige. He would leave soon and throw it away.

There was a pause of some seconds, broken only by a crossing of "Thanks" as they got things in order; then Blatchley lay back in his office chair and blew out the first whiff of smoke.

"I certainly do," he said more definitely. "Look at it this way. *The Confessions* has been out eight weeks and we have sold just over thirty thousand copies. That is pretty good, I know, and I'm extremely grateful to you. But that is the past. Now look at the present. By careful advertising I've induced the public to be really interested in the question as to Zoë's real identity. That's not going to last, my son. Somebody will do a murder or find out a home cure for corpulence. In half a week the chatty columns of the Daily will be full of something else. Every one who wants to has read Zoë and decided who she is. Very well, then. Now," and here he raised a podgy but dramatic finger, "this is the moment when we must say officially, 'The Author-Husband is Dash Blank.' In a moment the whole thing revives; every one is saying, 'I say, it *was* Dash Blank. I knew you were wrong. But what a show-up! What, not read it? Well, then, do.' The sales will leap up to the fifty thousand and nobody can say where they will stop. Without it, the book's dead." He stopped, dramatically sudden.

These were the only times when Geoffrey Alison shared Helena's ideas about the volume. "I'm very sorry if so," he said wearily, "but it's sold like anything and I expect it will. I still don't see why it's not cricket?" (He spoke more warmly now.) "I always warned you that I couldn't tell you who had written it."

"Bah!" The publisher waved that aside with a smooth fat hand which left a trail of smoke. "That's always so in the beginning, it's part of the game, but now it's in my interest, the book's, your friend's, your own as her adviser—I shall see you're mentioned as discoverer of the diary's great merits—in everybody's interest...."

Geoffrey Alison stood up abruptly. Each of these points had been emphasised by that fat hand; the office was the tiniest of rooms; and he disliked the smell more almost than the taste.

"I'm sorry, Blatchley," he said, as though bored with the whole affair, "but as I've told you half a dozen times...."

The man of business never fights a losing battle. "Of course, of course, my dear fellow. I understand. The feeling does you credit. Don't imagine I'm ungrateful. Not at all." He smoothed him with a diplomatic hand. His Zoë might write other books.

"Oh no, I don't," said the other dully.

"Look here," the publisher exclaimed, putting his cigar between protruding lips and drawing a note-book from a no less prominent waistcoat. "Why not dine with me one night to show there's no ill-will? I'm sure I owe you some commission! A little dinner somewhere gay, then the Empire or a supper—well, no details!—but what of something like that? Monday?"

"Thanks very much," said Geoffrey Alison more warmly. This was the sort of evening he liked, when some one else would pay. Then, suspiciously, in the old tones; "So long as you'll swear not to worry me any more about Zoë."

The publisher seemed hurt at this idea. "My dear fellow," he said, patting him again upon the back in a most soothing way, "what do you imagine? Business is business, yes," (he waved the hand once more expressively around his little office), "but pleasure's pleasure. Monday then: my flat: at eight."

CHAPTER XX
PLEASURE

Thomas Blatchley (which downright English names his mother and father did not give him in his baptism) was accustomed to boast that he was not an old-fashioned publisher. He wished of course to uphold the fine traditions of literature and so forth, but he believed in modern methods. He did not see that book-production had any essential connection with fine-panelled ante-rooms where authors waited in upholstered pomp. The modern plan was not to keep them waiting.

It may therefore be perhaps set down to his modernity of business spirit that he prepared to entertain his benefactor, Geoffrey Alison, with so much thoroughness. Here (he may be imagined to have said) was a man who had done him a good turn in business. Every care, then, must be taken to provide him with an evening exactly to his taste. Then, maybe, he might do him another.

However that may be, Geoffrey Alison was thoroughly delighted. Everything was just how he would have arranged it for himself, had he been a millionaire and not a struggling artist. When Blatchley, whom he really hardly knew, had first suggested this evening together, the programme mapped out had appealed to him; but safely home again, he had repented and been within an inch of cancelling. Yet was it wise to risk offending this man, a hard business devil, who already thought he was not playing cricket? ... So out he had come, mistrustful of the other's hospitality; with visions of Soho, and half expecting he would pay the bill.

Yet Blatchley, without any of that awkward "Where shall we dine?" business common to bad hosts, had instantly said; "Shall we try the Ritz?" as quite the natural thing. To this he had assented no less instantly, only regretting that he had decided against a white waistcoat. Then Blatchley had proposed the actual champagne he liked. Then there had come the Empire: two half-guinea stalls, in which they hardly sat, for Blatchley (who turned out to be a very decent sort) said he always liked the promenade much better than the programme. So they had sat about and had a drink or two, and laughed, and debated which of the beautiful ladies around them they should introduce themselves to without finally deciding upon any (exactly his own pet routine), and so on to the Café de l'Europe, where they had merely had a Kümmel and looked round a bit.

And now here they were at the Savoy, the proper end for any festive evening; with people, music, food, wine, light and everything exactly as it should be, and peace inside the soul of Geoffrey Alison. Blatchley was a dam good sort and not a business swine at all.

It would be untrue to say that Geoffrey Alison was drunk. No one is ever drunk at the Savoy. He was inanely genial. Blatchley was a dam good fellow....

"Well," said his host, as half the lights suddenly went out, obedient to a grandmaternal law of his adopted and free fatherland, "I think we must toast the lady to whom we owe this very pleasant evening!" He raised his glass, (they had worked back through brandy to champagne), and cried, mock-heroically: "To the unknown Zoë."

"My word, yes," answered Geoffrey Alison with a fat laugh, "I'll drink that!" He raised his glass and drank it off: no heeltaps.

The publisher had merely sipped the brim of his, but he filled up his guest's. "I dare say, my boy!" he laughed cheerily. "I dare say you will. I've my suspicions about you and Zoë."

"No, no," warmly retorted the other. He was so genial as to be nearly truculent. "I won't let you say that." He was not quite so sure now about Blatchley. "That's not right. She's a dam nice girl is Zoë, and she's as innocent as anybody makes 'em. I'm very fond of her, I tell you, and she's fond of me too." He pulled himself together in a very doggy way. "But that's all there is. I won't have you having suspicions. She doesn't know what all that means. I won't let you say that, Blatchley. She never thinks of anybody but her husband, damn him!" He looked very fierce indeed for a very few seconds: then he chuckled feebly. Dam conceited idiot, that ass Brett....

"I see," answered his host vaguely. He was waiting.

The other's swiftly-changing moods veered, the next moment, to suspicion. He gave a discordant laugh. "You're a clever swine, Blatchley," he said, with a sudden longing to strike this man flickering across the table.

"You thought I was tight! You thought I should give Zoë away. You want to know who she is, don't you? But not much! I'm less of an ass than you think, old man! Yes, that was it," he added in a sudden mood of contemplative depression; "you thought I was tight." All his anger had evaporated. It was a mere statement.

"Take more than that to make *you* tight," said his host, relapsing upon flattery as a safe weapon. He could afford to wait. They would not be turned out yet for a while and he had learnt already that Zoë was quite young, a girl. That ruled out many authors' wives....

But Geoffrey Alison was on his guard. An air of watchful cunning settled on him. He saw the game now, in his own fuddled way, and he did not mean to be drawn.

"Give it up, Blatchley, old man," he said so happily as not to be offensive. "Give it up. You won't get anything from me. I'm less of an ass than you think. You won't get anything from me."

He had flung his cards, bang! upon the table. The other took them up. "I hope you don't mean to imply, Alison," he said in injured tones, "I've stood you this evening just to pump your secret out of you."

"My dear fellow, my dear fellow," crooned Geoffrey Alison, stretching out a shaky hand to reassure the other's sleeve.

The publisher withdrew his arm with dignity, as one who did not intend to be patted by a man with those ideas. "It looks extremely like it," he said coldly. "I look on your remarks as damned offensive. Here have I stood you a pleasant evening—at least I hope so—from gratitude, and you attribute it to the most disgusting motives."

"My dear fellow," continued the other, who had listened to this with an open mouth suspended in the act of speech, "you misunderstand me." It came out with a rush, like one long syllable. "You misunderstand me entirely. We're gentlemen, both gentlemen. There isn't any question about anything like that. You utterly misunderstand me."

But Thomas Blatchley was not so easy to console. "It was rather hard, Alison, to understand what you said any other way."

"Look here, Blatchley old man: it's like this," said the artist, embarked now upon self-defence. "You're a good fellow, dam good fellow; very pleasant evening indeed; and I want to help you. But there's Zoë, you see; Zoë!" He laughed happily; then, more gloomy, "And there's Zoë's husband."

He sat gazing fixedly before him, as though content with having thus explained everything at last.

The great room was almost empty and yet more nearly dark, by now. A waiter who had stood anxiously close by, stepped forward eagerly, thinking that this pause would give him his chance. The publisher waved him impatiently aside with an oath easy to read from the lips.

"I don't see," he said, friendly once more, to his guest, "that Zoë's husband matters much."

Geoffrey Alison looked very wise. "Oh, but he does, you know," he answered. "He does matter. Mind you, I dislike him. Dam conceited ass. But he does matter," and he wagged his head.

"How?" asked the other, who saw the head waiter approaching. It was all or nothing.

Geoffrey Alison found that the question needed thought. "Well," he said very slowly, and there was only one more table-full for the head waiter to dislodge, "well, put yourself in his place, you know. All the dam papers with their headlines. Oh yes, he does matter."

"How headlines?" He could kill the stubborn ass. He knew that it was luck, not cleverness.

His guest, unconscious of all this emotion, aimlessly drew headlines high up in the air. "'Zoë mystery solved. Selfish swine discovered. Hubert Brett the author.' All that sort of stuff," he said, chuckling at his own journalistic readiness. "Oh yes, he does matter. Dam unpleasant for him."

"Well, I suppose so," answered Thomas Blatchley with resignation. "Ah, here's the chucker-out!" He pointed facetiously towards the splendid person now close on them. "We must go."

"A very pleasant evening, Blatchley old boy," his guest murmured without rancour, as he got up with excessive dignity and walked, grimly intent, towards the door. He was not drunk. Just genial....

As he undressed that night, he laughed suddenly, aloud. That swine Blatchley had thought he was going to pump him and in the end he had done nothing except pay the bill! Betray Helena, dear little girl? Not he!

He fell asleep, chuckling and with one sock on. People said artists were dam fools, but he had scored off a business man and got the better of a publisher....

As to Thomas Blatchley, he was far more calm. Success had long ago become a habit. He merely felt a little scorn for Geoffrey Alison.

This was by no means his first good stroke of business over two glasses—one full and one empty—of champagne. He was not a believer in mere whisky: stale, and not making towards confidence. No, a good dinner and then, at the end, quite conversational; "You know, your books don't get one half the booming they deserve. You made a mistake in not coming to *me*! I'd make an offer now; I would have long ago, if it was only cricket. And even now, old man, if ever...."

Of course it ran one into money. To-night, no doubt, had run him generously into double figures: but what might that sum not produce in interest? Business was bound to be expensive. You either went about or else you sat in a huge office. He merely spent on drinks what other publishers spent on glass-doors.

He wished, as he got comfortable for a well-earned night's rest, it had been some one better known than Hubert Brett.

CHAPTER XXI
EXPOSURE

"Both for you, sir!" said Lily with the air of an old friend, entering the drawing-room at nine o'clock two evenings later. She held out on a silver tray, the wedding gift of Kenneth Boyd, two letters. One was from Ruth and had been left, now, by the postman; the other, in the familiar green of the press-cutter, had lain in her pantry since the early post.

"Ah, a press cutting!" ejaculated Hubert.

"Splendid. How exciting!" Helena replied, as though delighted and surprised.

Lily went out. She did not even really want to smile by now. She had been in three places before this, and in each of them the husband had needed humouring in one way or another. She probably would never marry.

"It's very late," said Hubert expectantly. Two months had passed since the last straggling notice of *Was It Worth While?* and after this gap he could open his green envelopes without a sense of irritation; yes, even with excitement.

"The last one is sometimes the best, isn't it?" Helena threw the hope out soothingly, but from the corner of her eyes she watched him with a little nervousness. Certainly the most restful times were those like the last weeks, when there were no reviews. They did seem to upset him so. She wished now that she had opened this—except that she would never dare to give it him if it chanced to be good.

She wished this wicked wish a thousand times more strongly, half a minute later. Never, in these three years, had she seen Hubert so affected by a notice. Great veins swelled out on his forehead, till she was really terrified. She could pretend no longer not to notice.

"What is it, Hubert?" she asked as he said nothing. "I hope not a bad one?"

"This is too scandalous," he cried, half choked and speaking like a pompous old man in his anger. "Where will the newspapers ever stop?"

"What have they said now, dear?" He missed the tragic resignation in that one word "now."

"Read it," he said and thrust it almost roughly at her, as though blaming the whole world.

It did not seem, however, as though he could wait for her opinion. "Newer," "practically unknown," he fired out at intervals, and other adjectives.

But she heard none of them.

The paper swam before her eyes and every dim word filled her with a sick dread, a resentful wonder, an absolute despair, for this is what she saw:

"AUTHOR'S WIFE FIASCO

"OFFICIAL REVELATIONS

"Suburban tea-tables need buzz no more with questions as to the identity of that now famous Author's Wife whose recent confessions have raised such a pother. A representative of this paper found Mr. Blatchley, this morning, at last in an unbending mood.

"'The secret is out,' said the publisher, 'the author in question is Mr. Hubert Brett. The book, I may add, is naturally by his wife. There were reasons till now why her identity should not be divulged.'

"Those reasons will perhaps be guessed by all who remember the fierce controversy that raged recently and the big names that were thrown about, also the big sales. Whether these last will be helped by this official revelation will remain to be seen. The context had certainly prepared us for the wife-sacrificing author to be some one slightly better known. Mr. Hubert Brett is of the newer school of novelists, whose work is practically unknown to the bigger public. From *Who's Who* we learn that he has written some fourteen novels since 1899, and of these *Wandering Stars* is possibly the most familiar to library-readers.

"In this rather disappointing manner the Mystery of the Author's Wife leaves the select company of The Man in the Iron Mask, Jack the Ripper, Shakespeare, The Lady and the Tiger and other insolubles, to rank for ever with The Mango Tree, Fiona Macleod, The Englishwoman, and other mysteries which stupidly got solved."

Her eyes somehow deciphered the main points, and then she sat looking at the thin slip, seeing nothing.

"Practically unknown," suddenly came to her ears; "considering that *Wandering Stars* sold close upon six thousand!"

Then she heard herself speaking. "It's only a rag, not one of the real evening papers." She dared not say what she had got to say. She dared not face the storm. Hate, now, that was what ruled in her chaotic brain, hate and loathing for that treacherous, mean, little Mr. Alison. She knew she always had despised him, now—but he had been so kind.... Why had she trusted a weak man like him? Why had she ever written—married—been born—anything? Oh, what would happen now?

Her husband got up suddenly. That broke her tortured reverie, broke her inaction.

"Well, I shall write at once," he stormed. "Let's have the filthy thing."

She rose weakly to her feet and held it out to him. "What will you say?" she asked, still feebly trying to gain time, like men faced by a rope that they cannot possibly avoid.

"Say?" he repeated scornfully. "Tell them what they are and contradict the whole thing as a lie."

She almost staggered and caught hold of his arm. "No," she said. "Listen. You—you mustn't."

"Mustn't?" He looked curiously at her.

She suddenly burst into tears, clinging to him there as if for pity. "Hubert," she sobbed out, "don't take it as real. You're the best husband there could ever be. I wrote like you do. It was only——"

"My God!" he cried, clutching her arms roughly. "You *didn't* write it? You didn't——" He broke off and let go of her, holding her one moment at arm's length. She never could forget his eyes.

He stooped and picked up the cutting. He read it slowly through, as if that might help—or possibly to calm himself. Helena fell limply on the sofa. Minutes seemed to pass in silence.

Suddenly he crumpled up the little roll of paper and hurled it in the fireplace. Then he laughed and that alarmed her more than anything.

"Well," he said, trying to speak naturally, "that's that, then. It's no use having scenes, is it?" He stood very still, looking vacantly before him as though not realising what it meant.

"Hubert," she began again, as though in some way his name was a shield, and went to him, "let me explain——" but he waved her aside.

"What's the use?" he said gloomily. "It's all so obvious. The gutter Press has let itself go over me for weeks as the mysterious, self-centred Husband; the man who sacrificed his wife! I don't see why you should explain. It only makes things worse."

"But you don't see," she answered. "The husband wasn't you, any more than people in your novels. I wrote it—wrote it just for fun" (he snorted with an irony that even she observed), "never meaning the Press or any one—and then one day Mr. Alison——"

"Oh, *he* was in it?" Hubert asked with a swift passion. The old antipathy revived. That young ass always *had* been in it, somehow.

"He promised never to tell any one," said Helena. "You know, we wanted money so."

He laughed scornfully. "Oh yes, we wanted money. Money's everything. So long as we have money, what does it matter everybody knowing you think me a selfish brute or that——?" He broke off abruptly.

It was clear that he mastered himself only with an effort. "Have you *got* the book?" he asked with an icy calmness, presently. "I suppose as your husband I've the right to read it?"

She could not answer. Somehow she got to the door, to her own room; unlocked her jewel-case and took from it the loathsome little book in its clean, innocent, green cover: then she went down and handed it without a word to him.

"So this is it?" he said with all Scorn in the words. He opened it at random. "'I am the background,'" he read in slow, cold tones as to a child; "'the background for *his* work no less than the wall-paper of the one room where he can write; and I must be as quiet.'"

She stood there, thrown back fifteen years, a girl again before her governess: and he little suspected that with those words he was killing all her penitence and injuring her love.

"Anything sounds rubbish if you read it out," she suddenly blazed at him in quite another mood.

He shut the little book with a mild glance of surprise. "Don't let's have any scenes," he said once more. "This has just happened. It's pretty ghastly; don't let's make it worse. You'd better go to bed when you feel tired; I shall just sit and read—I want to know the worst. Don't wait up for me. It'd be rather a mockery to wish each other good-night!"

He moved towards the door. It was the time they always spent together, the best of her day.

She stood by the mantel-piece, leaning for support on it, wondering how any one could be so cruel—and feeling she deserved his cruelty.... It was so awful, put as he had put it: yet she had never meant——

His hand was on the door. She moved a few steps forward.

"Hugh," she cried, as though the name must surely explain everything: but he did not turn, even. He shut the door, quietly.

Helena threw herself face downwards on the sofa, but she could not cry.

CHAPTER XXII
THE IRON IN THE SOUL

To Helena the most terrible part about her husband's attitude was his astounding calmness. If he had but raged and stormed, she could have endured it. She might even have explained. What she could not bear was this chill resignation.

"We had better talk as usual in front of Lily," was all he said, coldly, before breakfast the next morning. "There's no reason why she should guess that anything is different."

"Must it be different?" she brought herself to say, though even that was difficult, with him like this.

As usual, he laughed contemptuously. "Do you expect it to be just the same, when I know, everybody knows——" He broke off. "Well," he said, "I suppose *most* married couples spend their time living up to their domestics. It's only we were lucky for a bit...."

They talked about the weather, then, and the day's news till Lily had gone out; he even called her "dear," but she could not live up to that: and when they were alone again, he gave a sigh which she interpreted to mean relief and finally retired behind his propped-up morning paper.

When he had finished breakfast—she ate nothing—he moved silently into his accustomed chair.

She moved across as usual to light a match for his after-breakfast pipe.

"No thanks," he said brutally. "I don't want to smoke. And I shan't work to-day of course."

She went out, hardened against such a foul attack, and half a minute later, from the next room, heard him strike a match....

Soon after eleven, when he had gone—work or no—into his own room, Lily announced Mr. Alison.

"Yes, I suppose so," she said dully.

He came in, very different from his late jaunty self, and threw a rapid glance at her, limp on the sofa. Her red eyes told their tale.

"You know then?" he asked. It was in some ways a relief.

She waited until she judged Lily to be safely through the swing-door: then she got up, by a natural instinct, and confronted him.

"I wonder," she said, "you dare come at all."

He looked anxiously about him. "Tell me," he asked almost in a whisper, "is he very sick?"

It was her turn to laugh contempt. "Oh, of course you think of yourself first! You're safe, though, here; trust him not to come near *me*!"

"No," said the other with an absurd dignity, "you wrong me. I meant, is he jealous?"

"Jealous?" she retorted in bewilderment. "No, why should he be? Of what?"

Geoffrey Alison suddenly found this difficult to answer and whilst he hesitated, feeling justly hurt, the storm was on him with its utmost force.

"I wonder," she said once again, for Man flies to a tag in moments of emotion, "I wonder you dare come and see me. I trusted you with all my happiness—with everything; you swore you'd never fail me; and now— —" She spread her arms in a pathetic gesture; then suddenly inadequate, a girl: "It really is too bad of you."

"Oh, come I say," he started. He had arrived full of shame and dread, realising from his newspaper that he had been tricked into a betrayal; but now that her onslaught was so tame—merely "too bad,"—he visibly regained his courage. "I think," he went on, almost aggrieved, "you might give me a chance of clearing myself. It's not my fault at all, it's that swine Blatchley. I dined with him three nights ago and utterly refused to say a word about it, but he tricked me somehow. I still don't see how the cad did it, but he must have because nobody else knew. I'm awfully sorry, Zoë— —"

That roused her. "Don't call me that," she broke in fiercely. "Never call me that again. As though I didn't loathe the name and everything it stands for! You wouldn't understand. It's wrecked everything, spoilt my whole life."

"Oh, come I say," he repeated automatically in a half-dazed manner.

"I hate it," she said, working herself up; "hate the book, hate everything to do with it, hate you. I wish to goodness I had never met you; then this never would have happened."

"Oh, come I say," he said a third time, still standing close beside the door, "I don't think that's fair. I only did it as a good turn to you. I thought it would be a new interest; you'd always so much time to spare; and then it might be useful too, the money— —"

"Oh, I know," she interrupted. "You meant well. People always do." It was an old cynicism new to her. She saw life wrecked before her feet—and here was the fool who had tried to help her.

"Well," he mildly summed up the whole case, "I can't do more, can I, than say I'm very sorry."

She could not even gain the relief of a real scene with this flabby nerveless creature. She turned upon him with contempt.

"No," she said, "you can't do anything of course! How could you? It's a great pity that you ever *did*. People like you aren't meant to—and I trusted you!"

"Well, what *can* I do then?" he enquired in hurt, plaintive tones.

"Go away," she blazed out, getting something like her chance; "go right away and never come near here again. Leave me alone to try and put the thing straight without your silly meddling. That's what you can do." She sank upon the sofa and took up a magazine with very shaky fingers.

"All right then," he said, recovering his dignity, "I will." He had a kind of feeling that Brett was sure to come in soon if this went on, and he should hate a scene....

"I will go," he repeated at the door, "and I'll tell Blatchley, now, to act direct with you." With this reminder of all that he had done for her, he went out very stiffly. She did not call him back, although so soon she felt half sorry for the silly little man. He had meant well and he was fond of her.... No woman finds it too hard to forgive a man whose sins are due to those two causes.

Helena, not so comforted by this scene as she should have been, sat with the magazine held limply in her fingers and wondered with a numb brain whether there was no way out of her life's labyrinth.

Hugh would not listen. That was the whole difficulty. If only he would let her speak, she knew she could explain. She loved him; they had had such jolly times; he wasn't in the least like Zoë's husband; she hadn't realised, till that first review came, that life in the two homes had been even similar; and if— —

Suddenly she gave a little happy laugh, the first for hours that seemed already months, then leapt up girlishly and ran to her bureau.

Of course! It was the very thing. Speaking was difficult, and somehow he always made her feel so young and nervous. But this was easy and he always loved things just a little different—what he called her "odd little ways."

Feverish with excitement, she sat down and wrote her Apologia:—

"MY OWN DEAREST HUGH

"(I *can* call you that on paper and in my own heart, whatever you say about speaking.)

"Let me explain. If you can bear how things are now, I can't, and I feel so terrible because although I meant absolutely nothing, I know it's all my fault. I *am* sorry, do believe that, go on reading, but not a word of Zoë is *me*, really honestly. It's just Fiction like your books, but it's the only sort of life I knew. Surely you can't believe I think of you like that? The Husband was imaginary, and I only did it in the winter, to pass all the hours while you were working. I never called it *The Confessions of an Author's Wife* at all, that was the publisher and people, and they never let me see it again till it was printed or I should have cut out a lot.

"Really, my own darling husband, *it was not my fault*. It's all very awful and I am so sorry for you, but don't let's make it worse by quarrelling ourselves. I'm sure we can live it down and nothing will be worse than if we're seen to have quarrelled. We will write a note together to the papers saying it was Fiction.

"Hugh, let me be forgiven and help you through this horrid time my *stupidity*, and that's all, has brought you to. You don't know how already I long to hear your laugh and just one kind word. We've not been sloppy, have we? but no one could be fonder or prouder of her husband, and I see so little of you anyhow. Don't rob me even of that. Come and tell me I'm forgiven and be your dear old comfy self again. I can't stand this.

"Your loving and Oh so sorry,
"H."

She read it over again, laughing through tears, for now everything would be all right. Then, when she had sealed it and was about to write his name, another idea came to her. He might tear it up, unread!

On the outside she wrote:

> To a very dear husband from a very
> sorry wife.
> *Quite short.*
> Read it!

By now she felt almost on the old terms—and how dear they had been, she could see now—with him. This was the sort of thing he always liked so much. It made him call her "child." She had sent notes before, when she had to go out or something.

Very quietly she went to his door, slipped the note silently beneath it, then with her bent finger gave it a good flick. She heard it whizz across the polished floor. He could not fail to see or hear it, as he always did.

With a new sense of peace she went back to the drawing-room and waited. She was ashamed to notice, in the glass, how red her eyelids were.

Did other wives spend awful hours like this or was it just that she was silly?

Minutes passed; the hour struck; the quarter; the half-hour.

He was not coming, then, till lunch time. What a slave of habit;—or was he trying to punish her by this suspense?...

She fought that last idea: it would not be like Hugh. Possibly he had written and left it in the hall? She went out. There was nothing there.

One o'clock struck, and almost instantly she heard his door open. She half rose, then she decided to sit where she was.

Would he never come? ... He was pottering about in the hall! Tapping the glass now! ... How could men be so curious? ... At last the handle turned. What were resolves? She could not help getting up, after all; but he must speak first.

There was no need, really. His set face told her everything. He did not come beyond the door.

"Helena," he said sternly, in a low voice that obviously considered Lily, "I think it'll be better if we don't discuss this matter any further. We may possibly forget. Anyhow, it's no time for childish games. I'd already written, as you suggest to the newspapers. We won't speak of this at all in front of Lily."

It was clearly a message learnt by heart, and with its last word the door shut. He had never let go the handle.

Helena stood gazing after him with a face no less set than his own.

CHAPTER XXIII
SECRET NUMBER TWO

Three days passed, seeming like a year, and everything was just the same. Each felt in the wrong, each had a grievance; and that is fatal for a settlement.

Helena, rebuffed, was quite determined to make no more appeals: and he was silent, that mockery of talk in front of Lily over, except that now and then he would throw out questions—with the hard air of counsel cross-examining—questions that showed upon what string his mind was harping, questions to do always with the hated book. These she answered patiently, as one who knows she has deserved her punishment.

What she had not deserved, what she would not endure, Helena decided, was his whole treatment of her. Each afternoon he had an agent, publisher, friend, somebody that took him into London; each night he had some work to do—and this although he told her brutally that she had fatally wrecked his new novel. It was a fresh routine.

Helena found herself sentenced—apparently for life—to solitary confinement in a new-art cottage. Callers arrived, suspicious in their frequency, but she said, "Not At Home" to all, caring but little to feed their taste for a tit-bit of scandal. Letters came too from dear friends who congratulated her ... but these she tore up, unanswered. Others came from Mr. Blatchley—unctuous, consoling, full of the glad news that sales were leaping up as a result, and sending a big cheque as a polite advance. Helena loathed herself for not destroying this as well; but she had sold her happiness, so why not take the price? Besides, if Hubert's new book had really had to be abandoned,——!

"I hope to get some reviewing work," he said at the end of the fourth ghastly lunch. "That will be something. I am off to town about it but shall be back to dinner."

She forced herself to speak in the same level tones that he adopted. "Doesn't it occur to you," she asked, "that it's not very pleasant for me, just now, to be always left alone? I can't go out like that, with everybody saying that we've quarrelled."

"Are you blaming me, now?" he asked in icy surprise.

She refused to argue this; she felt that it was mean. "What am I to do," she said, "all these lonely afternoons?"

"I should send for your good friend Alison," he answered with a grim humour, and went out to his own room.

Helena sighed, a sigh of despair; then she got up with more energy than during all these days, buoyed by a resolve.

Anything was better than inaction. Even a row would not be so awful as this freezing calmness! She would do something—must!

She took his advice. She went to the telephone and left a message with the Studio porter. She asked Mr. Alison to tea.

Then she went back to the drawing-room, and as she tidied the neglected flowers there was on her tight-pressed lips the whole eternal mystery of the sphinx-woman.

He arrived punctually to the moment—one second after the tea-urn— secretly nervous but outwardly full of a relieved delight. "I am forgiven then?" he cried, and she felt cheered already. It was something to talk. Besides, he really *did* look funny.... He laid on the table some roses he had bought and now had not the courage to present.

"I'm afraid I was a pig," she answered, nobly. One feud was quite enough for her. "I know you never meant to do it and you were awfully good about it all till then. You helped me such a lot."

"And I hope to do the same again," he said with an absurd little bow.

"Not give me away again?" she asked, mainly as a good excuse for smiling. But really she felt happier already. Tea smelt almost good again!

He looked at her with the reproachful eyes of a whipped hound. "You know I shouldn't, you know I never meant to. And I'm afraid you'll never trust me any more." He sighed cavernally.

"That's just what I'm going to do," she said, and then she could not refrain from laughing, for he looked so alarmed at new responsibility. "Oh, nothing like the other," she went on gaily, "this is a most harmless secret."

"What is it?" he answered keenly. "Tell me?" He hoped that Brett was teaing out somewhere.

"Well," said Helena, giving him his tea, "you know you said I ought to follow up the other with a second book and I said no? Well, now I think I will." She felt heroic and excited, merely saying it. It was her new resolve.

"Hooray!" cried Geoffrey Alison, catching some of the great moment's fire. "Blatchley *will* be bucked. He was immensely keen."

"Bother Blatchley," answered Helena. "I think he has behaved disgracefully and it is all his fault. But I can't stand this any longer; Hugh won't even speak to me; besides, if I write other books about quite different husbands, nobody can say they are all us."

"Excellent," said the other, grasping the involved idea at once, "and so——"

Helena laughed. "So now I'm going to write one about a woman married to an artist, and you must give me all the local colour."

"Shall *I* be Zoë's husband?" he asked eagerly. It still pleased him to say things like that.

"Oh no," she said, unconsciously ruthless, "no more than Hugh was the first; but I mean you must tell me what—well, what artists do."

"They paint," he answered gravely; and that made her laugh again. Ally was not a man to trust; she had been a real fool; but he was splendid company. He told her everything that artists did. He made her laugh a lot. Those endless hours of misery seemed nightmares of the past—until she was alone again.

But when business released Hubert Brett conveniently in time for their silent meal, he found in the hall a wife somehow less broken and submissive; less the girl-penitent serving a long sentence, much more a woman with secret laughter playing round the hard lines of her mouth.

"I'm glad you've got back," she said in the usual tone. "I took your advice and asked Mr. Alison to tea."

He had the sense to make no answer. But back in his study, he was weak enough to slam the door. And she was glad to hear it.

CHAPTER XXIV
BATTLE ROYAL

Geoffrey Alison felt very well content as he rang the bell and hastily fluffed out his hair. He was the bringer of good tidings and everything in general was going as it ought to go. Zoë was quite her old self again (would even let him call her that), had recovered from her silly temper, seen that he was not to blame, and now looked like making a bit of a stand against the conceited swine Brett, whom she had seen through finally.

He beamed on Lily, who remained impassive. There were, to her expressed mind, men and men. Mr. Alison, she had told Cook, was of the second kind.

"Is Mrs. Brett at home?" he asked.

"Mr. Brett, did you say, sir?" asked Lily. Humour is a wonderful assistance to those whose work is with the daily round.

"No; *Mrs.*," he replied, dwelling upon the sibilants in a way to delight an elocution-tutor.

He certainly did not want to see Brett, he told himself as Lily finally held the door open. He had not seen him since the crash, and fellows who had met him in the tube said that he was pretty surly. Geoffrey Alison did not like surly people—nor had he quite forgotten that scene in the garden.

Now whether it was that in his general delight with life he rang the bell with more than customary vigour and so brought out the owner of the house, or whether (as seems probable) there is some devilish telepathy that always tinkles into people's heads the exact thought one most wishes to avoid—whatever the cause, as in Lily's wake Geoffrey Alison stepped quietly past the study door this morning, it opened and Hubert looked out with something between suspicion and alarm upon his worried features.

Geoffrey Alison instinctively took a step backward.

The owner of the house, however, merely looked at him as though he had been dirt.

"Oh, it's you, Alison," he said, not holding out his hand; and then with an obvious sneer, "As busy as ever?" With which he put his head back and promptly shut the door. He might have acted thus if it had been the plumber—and he had wanted to change plumbers.

The other, naturally upset, poured this out instantly to Helena.

"Just like him, isn't it?" he said.

Helena would not be drawn to disloyalty, even about trifles.

"Hugh's such a worker," she said. "He thinks of nothing but his writing."

The artist, who was never busy, snorted. "He certainly does not think much about his wife," he answered. Extraordinary how a hog like Brett could keep the respect of a dear little girl like this!

"Well, what news have *you* got?" she enquired, to change the subject.

That reminded him. That scene with the great beast Brett had quite thrown the good news out of his head; but now, remembering, he won back his complacency.

"Capital!" he said, sitting down happily and pulling up his trousers to show light grey socks. Life was itself again. "Couldn't be better. What do you think? Guess."

"It might be anything at all, you see," she said with desolating common sense. "I never guess; it's only wasting time; so tell me."

"Well," began Geoffrey Alison, a little crushed, "I called along yesterday, after our talk, to tell Blatchley he had acted like a common cad."

"I don't see that's so very splendid," she objected. "You might have done it sooner, and anyhow he must have known that all the time. He only did it to get money, and he's getting it."

The other sighed, such a sigh as man has ever sighed when arguing with woman.

"You women *will* interrupt," he said loftily. Yes, they were quite on their old terms again.... "If you would only let me finish, I was going to tell you that he said he knew he had acted too hastily but that he hoped you would believe—and then he told a pack of lies, but here's the point." He spoke impressively. "If you'll let him have the new book, he'll pay you two hundred pounds down, only as a first dab of the royalties of course, and boom it better than ever, and he guarantees a still greater success, providing it's one half as good. So there, Miss Zoë, what do you think of your agent now?"

She did not exhibit the delirious gratitude which he clearly had expected. She sat, obviously thinking; and he for his part reflected that women were odd devils, however well you knew them. Surely nobody could know a woman better than he knew little Zoë; he saw more of her now than Brett did; talked to her with the direct ease of a husband—said just what he thought. Hadn't he just told her not to interrupt? Well, that meant knowing a girl pretty well; yet if any one had told him that she wouldn't be delighted about this book she wanted to write so much— —

"I shall have to ask Hugh," she said very slowly, breaking in upon his thoughts.

This was the last word.... Ask Hugh! Ask Brett, who had behaved like a damned swine about the other book, who wouldn't speak to her except to snub her, who thought of nothing except his own rotten work! The girl must be mad!

"Ask him?" he said in amazement.

"I ought to have asked him about the other," she merely replied. "Then everything would have been quite all right."

"Yes," he assented, mocking; "then you'd have never had your book out, never had all this success. Everything would have been quite all right."

"Yes," she said, seriously.

After this there was no argument. He could not bring himself to stay. It was so asinine. People must go mad when once they married! Oh yes, he could stay no longer. Ask Hugh, indeed, when she had got the chance of her whole lifetime! He could guess what Hugh, dear Hugh, would say.

"Well," she said, "if you must really go so early?" She had no suspicion of his mental turmoil. "And I'll let you know to-morrow about the new book, when I've asked Hugh."

But he had clapped his green hat on impatiently and strode away. He knew she would not listen to anything against her husband; she had such young ideas about that sort of thing; but really!— —

Helena, meanwhile, still innocent of the rage she had stirred up in him, spent the time till lunch in wondering how best to attack her not easy task. Before Hugh came in, she must have the book in its rough lines all in her head, so as to convince him that it was mere fiction and would make people believe at last the other had been meant for nothing more. Then he would surely not object, and be pleased; or if not—well, why worry about that? A row, she had decided, could not hurt like his cold silence. It would be human, anyhow. And what an outlet, what a boon for lonely evenings, the new book would be!

If war it must be, then let it be war; but she would do her best for peace.

When he duly entered, however, all her good natural openings and deprecating explanations were mere labour lost. He fired the first shot—and in quite a different campaign.

"Look here, Helena," he said, coming into the drawing-room and actually sitting down, though not, of course, near her, "all this Alison nonsense must cease." He clutched the chair-arm firmly.

"What exactly do you mean by that?" she asked, very calm; but inwardly her spirit veered decisively to war.

"What do *I* mean?" he snorted. "Surely it's quite obvious! Most husbands would be jealous, but I'm not like that. I know it's mere stupidity; I couldn't be jealous of a knock-kneed ass like Alison; but all the same——" In spite of himself he relaxed his hold of the chair-arm and got up, pacing hurriedly about the little room. "Look here, Helena," he said once again, more calmly, "I see through it all; don't fancy not, for half a moment. You women are so obvious. I know you think you've only got to make us jealous for everything to be all right, but it's not going to work here."

"I don't know even what you mean," she answered, rather as though he had just made a dirty joke.

"Well, *I* do," he thundered, "and I mean it, too. This has got to stop, I tell you. I asked you long ago, when—when things were different, to see less of this fellow. I don't trust him. I ran across him just now, and he cringed. Grrrr!" (and here he made a gesture as of one who washes hands). "It's bad enough that you and he should be about together, day and night, till everybody talks; but when it comes to a cad like that calling you Zoë and——"

"So you've been listening," she said. It seemed so easy to keep calm, now that Hubert was excited.

He laughed scornfully. "That's likely, isn't it? I heard him bellowing it out in the hall.... No, this has got to stop. It's bad enough to have the Boyds and all our friends here sniggering, but when the servants——"

She got up abruptly, and he sat down; the room was too small for two rovers.

"Perhaps," she began icily, "you'll let me say a word. You haven't let me for a week." He spread his arms, hopeless, and sat down. "I'm glad you're not jealous," she went on slowly, as to a child. "That'd be stupid. You know quite well that Mr. Alison is nothing but a friend. I couldn't respect him as——" but no, she wouldn't seem to beg for mercy; she broke off and spoke again in a much fiercer tone. "Perhaps though, as you've told me what I mustn't do, you'll tell me what I can. *You* won't come out with me, you shun me like a criminal, you only talk to me in front of Lily. Do you think I can live like that? Do you really think I'm going out alone, alone with the dog, and everybody saying: 'There's poor Mrs. Brett; she's in disgrace; he's punishing her'? No, I'd rather let them see me with Mr. Alison and let them think it's I who am avoiding you!"

He looked at her as at some strange being in his house. "Helena," he said, "this can't be you who's speaking."

"Isn't it?" she laughed. Then calming herself, "Perhaps then," she added, borrowing some of his irony, "if I'm not to go out with Mr. Alison, you'll tell me what I *am* to do."

"What do most wives do," he asked, "whose husbands are away? They don't rush about everywhere with artist-wasters; they do some work or something."

It was a vague ending, but it lent Helena her chance.

"Exactly what I wanted you to say," she cried. "I don't want to do anything again without your leave; but now I *will* do some work. I'll live my own life, if you don't want me to share yours."

"What do you mean, Helena?" he asked. This was a new mood.

"I mean," she said surprised at her own calmness, "that Blatchleys have offered me two hundred pounds advance for my new novel. I said I must ask you first, but now I shall accept it."

"I utterly forbid it," he cried wildly and leapt to his feet. They were both standing now.

"What?" she exclaimed. "Forbid? What do you forbid? How can you forbid? You could have, in the old days; I wouldn't have done anything if you had asked me not; but now—how can you forbid?"

"I do," he cried excitedly. "I utterly forbid it." He was gaining time to think.

There was a pause while they stood facing one another.

"Do you think," he said presently, "apart from all that's happened, this horrible publicity, my friends all chaffing me, I ever would have married the sort of woman you propose becoming? I wanted a wife to look after me, to be a nice companion; I didn't want a woman-writer. I hate that type of woman. You were a simple, jolly girl when I first married you, and now— writing this popular clap-trap!—you must see, Helena, it isn't fair?" His stern air melted almost to appeal.

She would not allow herself to listen but forced the argument on to a safer plane. "This one," she said, "has nothing to do with an author at all, there can't be all those terrible misunderstandings. Oh, don't you see, Hubert," she cried, "that if I wrote another book, all obviously fiction, these horrid gossips may believe at last the other was all like that too? Besides, it's stupid to refuse two hundred pounds just when you say things are so bad and we may have to move."

She had not meant it so, but this was her worst cut of all.

Hubert remembered his own failure; was reminded of her huge success.

A wife selling her books ten times as well as his own—a wife who wrote "for fun" in idle hours—a wife whom he had treated as a silly child.... "This one'll fail," he said almost fiercely, "it's bound to. You're nothing but an amateur, *I*'ve been at the job fifteen years. Two hundred's all you'll get, and much good may it do you!"

Full of conflicting moods; sullen yet ashamed; aware of his unworthy jealousy yet hardly able to endure the thought; sorry for her yet sick with his own wound; he turned away before the better side in him should win and he implore the pardon of this woman that he would always love, however much he hated her.

"Hubert," she began, aghast at his excitement.

"We won't argue," he said, back at the safe level of those days just past, and moved towards the door. She hesitated, not sure who had won.

At the door he turned. "Oh, by the way," he said, as to a servant. "I shall want a room for Ruth to-morrow. She's coming down before teatime."

Helena gave a short bitter laugh, which he just heard as the door closed.

She saw the issue of the tussle now.

He had failed to subdue the disobedient wife, and he was asking down his sister!

CHAPTER XXV
THE BROKEN TRIANGLE

Geoffrey Alison, bursting with anxiety for Helena's decision, found her next morning in exultant readiness.

"I accept," she cried excitedly, almost before he had got inside the door. "I accept Blatchley's offer. The book is growing splendidly. I've done two chapters and I see it all."

He thought he had never seen her in such good form, and he wondered. She had been so cold about it yesterday. He did not, of course, know about the meals between....

She could not, however, help telling him a little of it.

"Oh," she cried, "you don't know how glorious it'll be, having some work to do again; I've missed Virginia, I mean Zoë, horribly! It seems so endless, the day, now that Hubert's cross."

"Is he still sick?" the other asked. He only knew till now what people said. He was dying to hear, but she was so funny.

"Sick," she laughed mirthlessly. "That is a lovely word for it! He seems to be entirely different. I knew directly it came out, I had done something awful, but I thought he would understand and see I hadn't meant him really and forgive. But he gets worse and worse. I think his friends keep teasing him, and then he can't get on with his book in the least. It's sickening."

The artist was encouraged to a blow at his old enemy. "I expect really he's jealous of your success. He's always sensitive. He hates anybody his own age succeeding better." It was the first time she had ever said, or listened to, anything against her husband.

Helena was silent for a moment, dazed. Did this explain his harshness? Was he really jealous?

"Oh, I don't think so," she said, not letting herself think, for all the puzzling little bits began to fit, now, with a deadly ease. "I don't think it's that. He's naturally—'sick'!" and she forced out a laugh.

"I'm so sorry," he said. It was his first attempt at sympathy. Their talk had been on flippant lines.

She did not dare to look at him, remembering how funny he was when quite serious. "Thank you, Ally," she said gently. He was a good sort.

"*I'm* sorry," he repeated. "You know that, Zoë, don't you? I'm your pal, whatever Hubert is."

"Hubert's splendid," she said, childishly inadequate; and with these words, she who had been a hard woman for long days—melted perhaps by fatal sympathy or her own noble lie—suddenly found hot tears streaming down her cheeks. She turned away, ashamed, and hoped he would not see.

But he had seen.

What they had said just now had been enough—and this was far too much. Dear little Zoë—pretty little girl, too—married to that great swine Brett—in trouble—crying—wanting to be cheered.

The worst, of course, of keeping harmless vices as tame pets is that for years they only come out when needed and are very pleasant. Then, however, as time makes them stronger, comes the fatal moment when they gain the mastery, turn on their former owner and drag him where they will.

This was such a moment for Geoffrey Alison.

All those nice exciting stories, laudably abstract, bulked suddenly into the real. Here was a girl, crying—pretty too; dam pretty—and everybody knew that when dam pretty girls cried—why, they expected it....

"Zoë," he cried, surging forward, "why do you stand it? Why do you let him treat you like that? You're too good for him; I wish that I had half the trust, the love you give to him. I've done so much for you—the book and everything—and you're so hard to me."

An automatic thrill came in his voice, he leant a little forward; he stretched out timid arms towards her, ready to protect. There was no need to think; it came so easily. He had read the whole scene so often. The blood throbbed in his veins.

"My God!" he said, unthinking what it meant. They always did.

But Helena quite failed to play her part.

She got up hurriedly as his protective arms swayed over her; she backed and stared at him. He wasn't serious? She never knew....

Her tears had ceased. She felt a stupid terror. It was all so vulgar.

He dropped his arms slowly, chilled by her stare, and stood with his mouth ludicrously open.

"Oh!" she said at length, as though realising what the whole past had meant. "I thought you liked me—and it was only this."

They never had said that at all. He had no answer ready.

"Oh, come," he replied presently, "don't be so serious about it."

She spoke very seriously. "It was *my* fault," she said. "I ought to have seen. People told me. I thought you just liked me, and I suppose I was flattered. If only I had guessed! But I was always such a fool. You see, I never really had a chance. *You* taught me all I knew of art or anything. And that's why it's so terrible." The crisis over, she sank limply on a chair. She had never thought that anything like this could happen, ever. She knew it did in those books that she couldn't finish; but Mr. Alison——! He had been so amusing always; she had thought him a funny and kind little man. She had not even thought of any one but Hubert....

"Oh, come, you know," he was saying again. "Don't go on as though there had been a tragedy! That's the worst of you awfully innocent women; you always think any one means so much worse than he does. Why you'd imagine I'd suggested—well, almost anything; and all I wanted, just as my reward, was nothing but a kiss!"

Somehow, as he drew to an end of his halting apology, he realised how great the fall had been. Was this the man who had been almost throttled by a jealous husband? He felt, with a surge of self-contempt, that he had reached the level of a river-side tea-garden.

And to Helena, although far less consciously, the same feeling. It would have been better almost, less sordid, if he had meant something worse. A kiss—as his reward!... She understood why Hubert said "Grrrr!" and then washed his hands when he spoke about Mr. Alison. He was "funny" no longer; merely vulgar—vulgar and horrible.

"Please go," she said, more voicing her thoughts than meaning to speak. Then having started, she explained. "I don't want to be nasty; you've always been so kind; but it will be much better if we don't meet again. Hubert had asked me, anyhow ... and then, you see, I couldn't ever feel the same, quite, with you. Oh, I'm so sorry," she said, noticing his look—"but you do understand, don't you?"

"Oh yes, I understand," he answered, very deep down, and serious for once without seeming comic; "I've been a fool, a swine. He'd kick me if he knew—and he'd be right. But look here" (he could not keep away from his excuses), "do try to see it wasn't very much. Lots of women——" Then he caught her eye and said; "But you're so different and that's why I feel such a cad. Good-bye."

"Good-bye," she said and as he turned miserably away, she held her hand out to him, "and thank you all the same for what you've done. You've been a real good friend to me."

He had not looked for this and it was the worst part to bear. "I wish to God," he said passionately, "I'd been more worthy of your friendship. It's been the best thing in my life so far," and he turned hurriedly away, cursing himself for the damned fool he was. He had thrown everything away just for a moment that could never have meant anything. He had seen his real Self in her contemptuous eyes.

Helena stood, now, as the front door slammed, with eyes full of an emotion very different from contempt. She felt sorry—till her mind ranged swiftly back over all she had ever said to him, over the meanings he, a man like that, might read in it; and then she felt ashamed.

But all the while, unaccountably, she felt more alone than ever. She seemed so utterly thrown back on Hubert, now....

Presently, unable to bear the room's stillness, she went upstairs, mechanical as any housemaid, and busied herself needlessly about Ruth's room.

CHAPTER XXVI
TACT

Hubert at lunch made no reference whatever either to their own drawn battle or to that other, of which the sounds, she feared, might easily have reached him.

His one remark, indeed, beyond the usual polite abstractions for Lily's benefit, was "Ruth will be here at four o'clock. I want to see her before tea."

"Very well," was her submissive answer.

But this life of a housekeeper—how could she endure it after what had been? Hubert's only comments were aroused by letters, which his humorous friends still continued to send, quizzing him about his author-wife or sometimes facetiously alluding to some of the peculiarities of down-trodden Zöe's husband. "This I owe to you," he would say, throwing it across; or, "*You'll* enjoy this better," if a press-cutting contained nothing more pleasing to his vanity than a reference to himself as the notorious Husband.

Helena dreaded anything of this sort in front of his sister. She dreaded her visit entirely and hoped that it would not be long. Who could tell whether Ruth were not to be installed as her perpetual guardian, to watch over the wicked child? If so—but why make plans until things happened? The present was enough, and her chief wisdom lay in making the situation seem, to a third party, as easy as she could. She would *force* Hugh to speak.

There was a little fun in this idea, formed during lunch: and glancing across at his sullen face, with the too active mouth now tightly enough pressed, she only just restrained a laugh. It would have been the first during these ghastly and interminable meals.

So soon as he had got up, with his horribly polite; "Finished?" and the usual sigh, she ran almost lightly to the baize-door and called Lily.

"Lily," she asked, trying to compromise between an obvious whisper and a voice too audible, "were there any press-cuttings this morning?"

"Yes, mum," answered the always respectful conspirator.

"You kept them, I hope?"

"Oh *yes*, mum,"—almost hurt.

"Well, Lily," and she hesitated, the coward of Conscience; "I think I'll have them now and not to-night. Miss Brett will be here then."

Lily retreated and came back with the small envelope. Her eyes glistened sympathetically in the half-darkness. Perhaps she guessed—but she knew her own favourite among the Bretts.

Helena with that delicious thrill which makes crime so popular a hobby among those unable to afford sport or collecting, went into the drawing-room and boldly tore open the envelope addressed to "Hubert Brett, Esq." She did not want unpleasantness in front of Ruth.

She spread the cutting out, to read. He had not published a book now for months, so it was certain to refer to hers.

It did.

It was from *People And Paragraphs*, (which its admirers call by its initials,) and it ran, in the crisp, breezy, style which makes that sheet so popular:

"TURNING THE TABLES.

"Many a woman finds herself socially snuffed out by being wedded to a luminary: she is Mr. Dash Blank's wife *et voila tout*. There have been cases exactly opposite; but hist! They say the lady herself is now touchy on the point. It cannot often have happened, however, that the tables have been turned so neatly as in the case of the Hubert Bretts. As a novelist, he has for a decade of years formed one of the small and essentially select *coterie* that largely exists, like the ladies who lived on each other's washing, by patting one another's backs. His reputation has been large, his notices extremely good; but neither adjective would fit his sales. Any librarian (librarians, *en passant*, are interesting men) could throw an odd light upon the curious relations between

REVIEWS AND ROYALTIES

"Now mark the sequel. Pretty little Mrs. Hubert, bored with her husband's neglect, indites a diary, which a keen-sighted publisher gives to the world. Hey presto! as dear old 'Bertie' Zoda used to say at the never-to-be-forgotten Pen-Pushers' Saturday nights (or were they Sunday mornings? Tush!), in a moment all is changed. She sells fifty copies to her husband's one;

the book is in everybody's hands and mouth; the next is eagerly awaited—and poor Hubert finds himself, after all these years of manly efforts, as nothing more glorious than Zoë Brett's husband. Rough luck, Bertie, very!"

With a feeling of almost physical sickness Helena realised how narrow had been the escape. If he had read that, with his sister there——! She tore it viciously across and across, until no hand could ever piece it back to its vile self again. She felt the very action a relief.

In future, so long at any rate as Ruth was with them, she would open and destroy all cuttings. They could refer to nothing but her book. She went along and told the still impassive Lily to keep them all for her. She waited, this done, for Ruth Brett's arrival with far more complacency. At any rate her eyes weren't red....

It is typical of Hubert Brett's peculiar temperament that he had never thought of Ruth—at any rate as guest—until he needed her. He had marked her birthday down in his small pocket-diary, so soon as he bought it each year, and never failed to send a cheery note, however busy; and the same at Christmas. Also, when she had written letters filled with endless details about people he had never met and clearly should dislike, even if he had not read them all, he left no single one unanswered. But for the rest, she had her little cottage on the Norfolk coast and he his little home; so why should either trouble with the other? Many people sacrificed their life to relatives!

When, however, Helena grew so defiant over this affair which had been her own fault entirely, he thought at once of Ruth. She had been always full of doctrines of submission—almost maddeningly so; *she* saw that women who lived with men who were busy should be considerate, unselfish. She would not, he knew, approve of Helena's idea that she should be an author too, neglect her wifely duties and become a rival to himself. Ruth had been tiresome, certainly, in her persistent martyrdom, but she had never done a thing like that.

As for Ruth Brett herself, she did not question her brother's command. There is a lot in habit; besides, she happened to be fond of him. She took the train, directly she received his wire, and came. She hoped that it was nothing serious. He might have told her—but he wouldn't think....

She had met Helena so few times; Hubert had kept them apart in the old days; but now, so soon as the young wife stepped out into the hall, she flung herself upon her and cried, "What is it? Is he ill? What has happened? Quick!"

Helena was overwhelmed. She had rehearsed so many meetings—always with one idea: to seem at ease in an united home—and none of them of course was right.

"Oh no, he's all right," she said in confusion. How could she explain? "He wants to see you first. In there!" And the bewildered Ruth, scarce entered, still with her umbrella, was thrust at once towards another door; leaving Helena with the reflection that after all things had not turned out too badly, even though all the rehearsals had been absolutely useless.

Hubert jumped up from his table with a cry of welcome.

"But Ruth!" he said, holding her by both arms, "what's happened? I should not have known you." He did not realise the difference which changed environment can make in the chameleon, Woman.

"Well, it's three years," she explained.

"But you look ten years younger!" he cried, laughing. Just for a moment he forgot his troubles. It was incredible, this new Ruth with firm cheeks and bright colour; gayer even of costume. He could not understand—and he was little used to that. "I know!" he said; and then accusingly; "Ruth, you're in love."

At once a little of the old-time pathos crept into her face.

"No," she replied, "I think I've left all that too late."

"What is it, then?" persisted he, manlike.

"It's Norfolk," she said. Not for a million pounds would she have told him it was Freedom.... "Tell me, Hugh," she added quickly, "what has happened? Why did you wire for me? Everything seems quite all right!"

"Everything is utterly all wrong," answered Hubert, finding some consolation in a saying so tremendous; "it couldn't possibly be worse," and he poured the whole story forth with the accumulated passion of a week's not easy silence. How many times he had rehearsed his grievance to himself—when he felt any danger of relenting!

She listened to the end, attentively, in silence, and as she listened, it occurred to her too that these three years had wrought a miracle of change in her. All this, that he was hurling forth indignantly, seemed to her now so tragically small. She realised the pathos of a life in which—as with her, in the days gone by—one sense of wrong after another would always wreck his happiness and wreck the life of any one he loved. It had been her; now it was Helena; there always would be, must be, a victim to his tragical self-centred brooding. And he would not be happy, ever. He would stand alone upon the dignity of his achievement; alone, he would distress himself that nobody considered his work, him; alone, upon his deathbed, he would understand too late that he had never lived at all.

She looked at him with pity as he ended, the tempest lulled by its own blown-out fury.

"Well," he said presently, as she was silent.

"I can't understand," Ruth answered slowly.

"Can't understand?"

"I haven't read the book," she said, "our village library does not believe in modern fiction, but—well, what I don't understand is this. You say *she* swears the husband wasn't meant for you. Well, then, from what you tell me of his character in the book—weak, selfish, bloated with conceit, a little man who thinks he's great, full of absurd cranks about 'atmosphere' and so on, cruel to his wife—I wonder *you* can ever pretend, or care to pretend to think that it was meant for you! You surely don't think three years have made you like *that*?" and she gave a laugh as at some absolute absurdity, confident in her own knowledge of how splendid a man he had always been.

He looked up swiftly. He suspected her. But she did not flinch, for this was a new Ruth indeed. She looked straight at him—puzzled innocent surprise—and it was his gaze that fell after all. He knew what she meant—and she knew also that he knew.

The woman's tact had conquered in a sentence.

"Anyhow," he answered sulkily, acknowledging defeat in that one word, "you must see *she* is in the wrong? I know you women always hold together, but you must see that it's not—well, not exactly pleasant for me to be paragraphed in every rag as the selfish author-husband, whether I was meant or not. She had no right to publish it without my knowing."

"Oh yes," assented Ruth, "I see that, quite. She has been very silly, but I'm sure she meant nothing and perhaps——" Then she stopped abruptly and repeated; "But she has certainly been silly."

Hubert, oddly full of guilt and humiliation, was glad to leave this interview at such an end. He had planned it in a way very different.

"Well," he said decisively, as he got up, "I can do nothing with her. She persists that she will bring another book out now, and so revive the whole unpleasant business! Tea will be ready and you must want it, but afterwards" (he touched her lovingly upon the arm), "I know you'll want to help me, dear old girl. You'll go and talk to her quite firmly, won't you?"

"I'll go and talk to her, yes," said Ruth, pressing his arm no less fondly.

He did not notice that she dropped the adverbs.

CHAPTER XXVII
THE TWO WAYS

It was not a comfortable meal, this tea, and though Helena no less than Ruth knew it to be the prelude to a scene, neither could feel much regret when Hubert with clumsy ill-ease said; "Well, it is five o'clock, I'll leave you two to a chat," and so out, colliding with the door.

They were left staring at each other, the wife and the sister.

Helena, although she knew the object of this chat and the whole visit, could not work herself up to the pitch of feeling so much resentment as she had intended. This was such a different woman, who looked across at her with bright understanding eyes, from the one she remembered: shrivelled, worthy, with a hint of tracts to come. Helena looked back across the fireplace at her almost with a smile.

It was Ruth who spoke first. "Well," she said, "of course you know I've been asked down to make peace."

It was so unexpected that Helena did actually smile. "To make me a good girl," she emended.

"I'm afraid," laughed Ruth, "as usual with children, you are both to blame."

It all seemed easy in a moment. Helena suddenly felt the thick clouds of misery lift from her soul. She believed in Ruth. The whole air of the little room appeared to change from stiff hostility to friendly hope. Tea seemed a thousand years ago. She gave a cheery little laugh.

"Look here," said Ruth, encouraged, "I'm so glad you're taking it like this; I hated coming down. I know how people feel about in-laws and I thought you'd think I had come down to side with Hubert blindly. I've not, a bit. I'm very fond of him, but I see all his faults. I only want him to be happy. I'm forty, you know, and I've seen a good deal of things, so possibly——"
She broke off and said, by an abrupt change; "You see, I lived with him for

years and years so I can understand. He's difficult, I know, when you're with him, but when you get away—isn't he a dear?" She smiled.

"He's *more* than that," said Helena, suddenly wanting to cry.

She had said it unthinking, moved by the other's appeal, but to Ruth it was everything, for it meant that her task was easy. She embarked with confidence.

"When I first lived with him," she began, "I met a lot of well-known writers, artists, actors. He used to go out more then, and it flattered him to meet men who were famous. Well, I came to the conclusion that the greatest men are the most tragic, the most pathetically childish. I suppose you *have* to be self-centred to succeed; and then somehow, they can't get used to the little things. You know how press-notices upset poor Hubert? Well, they're all like that about something or other. You see, you married a man of that sort and you must make allowances."

"Oh, I do," said Helena, leaping at self-defence. "I always did. It's *him*. He won't forgive me, won't believe I'm sorry, won't let me put things right. You don't know what this week has been. I can't endure it, really."

"And so," asked Ruth, "you mean to write another book?"

Helena for just one moment scented battle and replied more stiffly. She would not throw her arms down till she knew there was to be no fighting. "What do you expect me to do, otherwise? He won't allow me to see other men, won't talk to me himself. A little house like this is nothing. What am I to do? It isn't even as though I'd a child."

Ruth answered very slowly. "Hugh is just a child," she said with a great tenderness.

Helena laughed. "A child indeed? If you could have heard him this week!" She suddenly grew hostile. "Why," she demanded passionately, "should everything in the house hinge round *his* career? Why am I not to write another book? Is it because I am a woman? Mine has sold better than all his put together and yet I'm not to do another! I'm just to sit at home, here in this tiny room, while *he* works and says we've no money! No, I utterly refuse. I've got an offer and I mean to take it."

Ruth looked troubled, feeling that she had been confident too soon.

"Helena," she said very gently, thrusting the name forward to make peace, "I'm not going to ask you to give up your career; I'm asking you to spare Hugh his illusions."

"I don't see," answered Helena, suspicious.

"No," said the other, and then paused. Helena thought that she had finished, when she suddenly began again. "I've been alone a good deal these three years, and I have thought a lot about marriage. Oh, not for myself, no" (she spoke so sadly that Helena relented for a moment); "but because my life now is so different from the one I spent with Hubert, and that makes one think. You know, if I'd my life to live again, I'd live it all alone—I'm afraid, yes, I'd sacrifice Hubert: men are born to marry, not to live with sisters!— but I'd have my life-work."

"And yet," swiftly interrupted Helena in triumph, "you ask me to give up mine?"

"I don't." She spoke decisively. "I only ask you not to sacrifice Hubert's to it."

"I still don't understand." Her voice was almost resentful.

"Hubert married you," began Ruth expansively, "because he is the sort of man who needs encouragement. He wanted some one who'd think his work wonderful and ask him how he did it. You surely see the difference? Imagine his life now, for any one like him: your bigger sales, your long reviews, your photographs, his own eclipse. It is impossible."

Helena remembered the press-notice and spoke more obediently. "What are you asking me to do then?"

"Leave him." The words dropped out like heavy weights.

"Leave him?" cried Helena, and by a natural dramatic instinct she rose from her chair. "Leave him when I'm fond of him?"

Ruth looked very earnest. "Leave him," she said again, "unless you're fond enough of him to give up your career. I tell you—I *know*—you can not have both, with Hubert."

"You cannot serve God and Mammon," murmured Helena. She did not know that she had said it. She sank down into her chair again and forced her numb brain to thought.

"Don't break all his illusions," she heard Ruth saying, miles away. "Be gentle with him if you're fond of him. You know how sensitive he is. Your books, you say, sell better. How do you think he could ever endure that, he who—I tell you—is nothing but a child? It would be agony, a life-time agony; disgrace. He lives upon success, on admiration, on being the centre even of a little house. How could a man like that endure to be just Helena

Brett's husband? ... Oh no, you won't do it, you can't be so brutal. No one can forbid you your career, but go away and work it out alone. *I* will look after Hubert, if he needs me."

That struck home, among these words that came dully to Helena through the chaos of her thought. "So that's it," she said with a bitter laugh, longing to hurt somehow. "You're thinking of yourself."

"God knows," said Ruth solemnly, "I wouldn't come back willingly for half the world, fond as I am of Hugh. I've *lived* since I got right away alone beside the sea. He always trampled on me; I lay down; I haven't got your courage. I often cried myself to sleep—and he not even guessing he had been unkind! It was hideous, I see now; hideous every day of it. But I'd go through it all again, and worse, sooner than expose him to this agony."

There was conviction in her tones. Helena tried to arouse herself. "Leave him?" she said dully. "Surely there's some other way? Even if he didn't mind, think of—— You talk about agony, but how can you advise me to do this, when you know how his friends——"

"Nothing would hurt him," said Ruth earnestly, "nothing in all the world—that is the awful part—so much as this blow to his pride, this shattering of all his life-work. He thinks—he told me so—he thinks this book of yours was just a fluke, an amateur attempt; that you can never do another. Oh, don't you see?" (she cried impatiently): "Must I put it in words? He thinks that *he* is a real author, you just nobody; that *he* has studied, he has nerves and everything an artist has, but you are just a woman. He lives upon his self-conceit.... Oh yes, I've said it now; I had to. It's not disloyalty. I'm fond of Hubert too—everybody is, because he is so thorough in it, such a perfect child. And everybody spares him too. Men of his sort are never told; everybody pities them the shock. They smile on him and like to see him so contented. They call him 'dear old Hubert.' It's half pity, yes—but also it's half love. I've seen it all so clearly since I got away. I've sometimes told myself that if I had those years again, I should let him have the whole truth; but I know that I shouldn't. And *you* won't either, Helena. Nobody ever does. They dream on happily, and all we others seem the selfish ones to them. It's all a comedy, when you're not near enough to see the tragedy. I've thought a lot about it, and I'm so glad now I was gentle. And *you*'ll be gentle too, I know. You'll either go away or you won't write: it's not for me to settle which; but you'll be gentle. You said just now you hadn't got a child. You have. No married woman is without a child. You won't be hard, I know, will you, because your child has been a little spoilt and things have suddenly gone wrong, and—just for a little bit—he loves to hurt his toys?"

"I—I never thought of it like that," said Helena, an odd look in her eyes. "I thought him so splendid and clever, so terribly above me. It all seemed so hopeless."

For answer Ruth went across and kissed this girl who made her feel so old. "I wish we had known each other sooner," she said. "I must go and unpack."

But outside in the hall she stood for a few moments, dabbing at her eyes with a quite fashionably small handkerchief.

CHAPTER XXVIII
WOMAN PROPOSES

Ruth had abandoned her pleading at a clever moment, for she had left Helena with a sense of pity, and pity means more to a woman than conviction.

Poor old Hubert! She was glad now, oh so glad, that she had spared him. It had been on her tongue yesterday, when he was so contemptuous about her book being popular claptrap, herself an amateur, to answer: "Well, I have found out about your own work too: it tries to be popular and isn't,"—to tell him she had also learnt that one could write without upsetting the whole household by one's fads and poses.... But in the end she hadn't. Perhaps it was as Ruth had said: every one would always spare him. Something, in any case, had held her back, and now she was glad; for that once said, it would have been too late. She felt that Ruth had spoken truly: he never could have cared for her again.

Poor old Hugh!

Buoyed by this feeling, crushing under it all others, she went to her bureau and unlocked the drawer where she kept her secret manuscript. There were three chapters. She would destroy them before her mood changed. Then she would go to him and say that he was right, she was not clever in the way that he was—she was an amateur. He would take days perhaps, yes even weeks, before he could forgive her quite; but it was as Ruth had just said. The rivalry gone, he would soon learn to bear the rest. He would have won back his self-sufficiency, ... poor Hugh!

She took out the written sheets with all the feelings of a mother who sacrifices her own son, touching them gently as if even in this last hour they had been something sacred.

Then—weak if you will, but do not be too hard upon the-Mother-soul—then she began to read.... just a few sentences.

And as she read, the whole thing leapt to instant life; began to grow, as poor Virginia had grown. She saw the painter, strong in a way—not Geoffrey Alison at all—but with a fatal vanity. Yes, that would be his fall, of course. He would be all right with the women he admired; there were so many, he was safe enough: but when he met the woman who admired him— —!

She had not thought of it like that before. She did not know where the idea had come from now. Before it went she hurriedly seized up her pen, to add a note to the confused synopsis.

Then she remembered.

What was the use if she was just going to destroy it?

If— —!

And its constant sequel: Why?

Why should she destroy her work?

It was her work no less than Hubert's work was his, however much more easily she worked. That hers came to her brain, she knew not whence, whilst he hammered out his from formulæ, was very likely nothing much against it.

Why had he said this second book would never sell? It interested her: why should it not interest others? How could he possibly know, when he had never seen it?

It was mere jealousy of course.

Ruth had said practically that. She had said that he could not endure rivalry; he must be supreme, if only in a little house. He knew that her book had sold better, ever so much better than any of his own, and that was what he really minded. Yes, she saw it all now; all from the beginning. He had not minded in the least that she should think him (as he still believed) self-centred, cruel, or neglectful; that had not pained him in the least, he had not really minded her publishing the book. No, what had really hurt him always—she saw now—was the book's success; what Ruth had called his own eclipse. He had worked, as he said, for fifteen years; he had called it a "job"; and in one moment she had cut him out!

That, Helena decided in a rapid flash, was the whole mainspring of his anger.

And was she to sacrifice her work to satisfy the petty vanity of such a man? Was she to admit her failure, to feign life-long admiration for his work, when she knew that with practice she could almost certainly do better?

No!

The answer came decisively.

As if to clinch it, she thrust the manuscript back in its drawer and turned the key with a decisive twist.

She would not sacrifice her own career to his conceit. He had spoilt Ruth's life, used her as a housekeeper until she was too old for anybody else; then turned her out—and now he thought he could spoil hers. And every one would spare him, because they were sorry! Why should she spare him? Why should she be sorry?

Helena stood with her fingers still upon the key, transfixed by the enormity of this new thought.

Why should she either smother her ambition or else creep away, sparing him the reason; leaving Ruth to be his victim once again?—poor Ruth, emerging into life again, escaped from this vampire who had left her an old withered woman at the age of forty.

No, she would not. Others might spare him; *she* would tell the truth.

She would go now, whilst Ruth was upstairs, and would tell him what she, what Ruth, what everybody thought. She would tell him that he was murdering the love of those who loved him by his own selfish blindness; that all this nonsense about moods and inspiration was mere pose, that you could write quite well wherever your two candlesticks were put; that every one saw through him but himself; that he should be proud of his wife's success, not jealous, if he had a spark of decent feeling in him; would tell him she too was ambitious, though a woman, she too had a life to live; that she was bored all day, with him at work, and now she meant to have her own work too; that Zoë had been right—yes, had been Helena, Helena not then but Helena as she was now; that she saw now, as Zoë had declared, she had been nothing but a background to his work. Now that was over and she would sacrifice herself no longer.

Oh yes, and she would tell him the rest too—that she was fond of him, would always be; admired him for his strength as much as she despised the flabby Mr. Alison of whom he had been jealous; that she would try to make him happy, comfortable and happy, not neglect the house; and they would be proud of each other's work, and even if she was not a success, her little earnings would all help to pay those horrid bills.

And if this did not satisfy him, if he could not live like that—well, then, there was what Ruth had said....

When he had heard the truth, the choice should lie with him! He might choose then between the sister and the author-wife. But they must have the truth. She would not sacrifice poor Ruth to him again. He had been spared enough already. The truth would make him happier. What could a man so selfish know of happiness?

Poor Ruth, contented with her mission, laying on her bed a dress that would astonish Hubert by contrast with the prim grey horrors of old time, little guessed how too thoroughly she had let in the light to Helena's young eyes!

Helena released the key and moved with firm resolve into the hall. She dared not stop to think. She strode across the narrow carpet and boldly turned the handle of his sacred room at this forbidden hour. She did not even knock.

There is much courage in a symbol.

CHAPTER XXIX
HELENA BRETT'S CAREER

Helena stood at the door, as on the day when she had lost her watch; and now again each detail stamped itself instantly upon her brain.

But this time Hubert was not working.

He sat at his desk, his hands stretched forward to hold open a paper laid before him. Helena even observed the wrapper from which it had come, rolled up quite tight beside the blotting-pad. She saw Hubert's air of rapt attention and noticed that he had not heard her enter. She saw two letters unopened on the table, and she thought how like him it was to open first a paper almost certainly sent him because it had some mention of himself. Yes, she could see now the blue pencil marks beside the paragraphs that he was reading. And they were exclamation marks....

Then, last of all, she recognised the paper.

It was *People And Paragraphs*—and he was reading that comment on the Hubert Bretts! She had destroyed the cutting; never thought of his dear friends.

In one moment all the words rehearsed died on her tongue. Afterwards perhaps, but for the moment she must comfort him. She could not hurt him more just now.

"Oh, Hubert," she cried, running to him and putting her hand impulsively upon his shoulder, all forgotten save the instinct to console, "they haven't sent you that?"

He turned round with quite a dazed look, apparently not in the least surprised to see her there. "Oh yes," he said in a hard voice, "there'll be lots of those. It's only just beginning." He stared dully at the spiteful, vulgar, words.

She knew what they must mean to him and once again her soul veered round to Ruth's mood of pity—pity and regret. It was her fault, this, she knew that; he had been right all through. He was so right and strong, and that was partly where her anger lay. She could have forgiven a weak idiot like Ally better.

She looked down at him; wavering, torn by two instincts, doubtful.

She looked. She could not see his face, but on the blotting-pad there dropped two tears.

She had not known that men could cry. Those two damp spots that spread on the green pad beneath her fascinated eyes told her of what his agony of tortured pride must be—and brought back to her memory those words of Ruth's; "He's nothing but a child: be gentle."

He was *not* strong and right. He did *not* have a soul of iron, this man: *not* despise her as a weakling. He was weak himself. He was a child and wanted sympathy....

Some other words of his came drifting back to her as she stared blankly at those spots of darker green and he sat with his head averted—was it in anger or in shame?

He never would have married a woman who wrote: hated clever women! All that came back to her. Had she played fair? He wanted somebody to help, encourage; could she be his rival? For better, for worse— —

Suddenly she found herself talking.

"Hugh," she was saying, back on the words of a yet earlier rehearsal, "I'm so sorry. I've been such a beast, and I *have* wanted so to do the proper thing. I've been a beastly wife to you, and now I've come to say you're right. I can't finish the new book; I can't get on at all." She paused and said deliberately; "I'm just an amateur."

And in one moment, before she had finished, he was on his feet. He had his arms round her with all of his old love, and held her at arms' length, and looked at her with pride, as though she had just spoken of anything except her failure.

"Darling little girl," he said, "don't, don't, you make me feel so bad. Don't say you've been a beast. Do you think *I* don't know what I've been to you? Do you think I don't know how true the whole book was?"

She smiled back at him, and he never saw the little bitterness or pathos there was in it, as she heard his old word of tolerant affection—"little."

He had not used that word for ages....

He drew her to him and kissed her very lovingly. "Oh, Helena," he murmured, close beside her ear, "if only you knew how I've missed you, how miserable I've been, how I have loathed myself. You splendid people think we horrid selfish beasts don't realise our vices. Oh yes, we do though, those of us who think, but we hope no one else observes them. I knew that

I had bullied Ruth, sacrificed her life to mine, and I vowed when I married you—but what's the use? You never change your nature, and I'm just a selfish swine."

"Don't say such awful things, Hugh," she said gently.

He laughed. "I'd say them for ten years as penance if it did any good. But now you've told me, now I know you know, it's easier. When I get selfish, when I begin forgetting *your* side of the thing, you'll have to tell me; see? And if you don't, well I've still got your copy of *The Confessions of*— —"

But she stopped his mouth with a kiss. "Hugh," she cried, going to the table and taking up the paper which had changed their lives, "we'll never mention that vile book again, and as for those who do"—she tore the paper savagely across. "And you must *not* say you are selfish. It's only that your work— —"

"My work!" interrupted Hubert, with a discordant laugh. "I've done none this last week. I've thought—thought about myself, and that's good when you're forty but it isn't pleasant. Do you know what is wrong with me?"

"Nothing," she said gaily, for he spoke with a cavernous gloom and she desired to change his mood.

He utterly ignored her. "I took a long time finding myself out," he answered. "That's all. Everybody starts, about eighteen, thinking he's a genius and bound to end up on Olympus; then about twenty-five, we settle we're just common fools and take a city job. But I did not. I've gone on in what they call a fool's paradise; feeding upon praise and threatening those who did the other thing, until I really thought that I was some one great! Boyd always *said* that I was undeveloped; there was something lacking.... But I've got it now. I think I got it when you cut me out as author!"

"Don't, please," she cried, "you mustn't talk like that."

"I must," he answered gloomily. "I've given half my life to writing— and only just found out that I can't write!"

She came to him then. "Look here, dear," she said, taking his arm in quite a mother's way, "you're just beginning your success. Men never *do* succeed till forty. You've just found yourself. You're going to do splendid things and you will let me help."

"What? You and I collaborate?" Was there a tinge of the old-time suspicion?

"No," she said quickly. "I shan't ever write again; that's done with; we'll just talk the stories over when we're out upon our dear old rambles, and then, you see, you'll get the woman's view as well. And possibly I may get plots sometimes, although I couldn't write them."

"Then we'll sign Helena and Hubert Brett," he said in swift penitence, forcing himself to nobility. "That really does sound excellent!"

"No," she replied slowly, "you must always sign. You see your name is known. Helena Brett has never written anything, and Zoë Baskerville is dead—thank goodness!" She forced herself to smile. She must remain the amateur! That touch of pity, she knew, must be there if things were ever to be right again....

Perhaps he guessed a little, for suddenly he clasped her in his arms again. "My God, Helena," he cried passionately, "how insignificant and mean you make me feel! You women can forgive, and we're so obstinate. You've spared me such a lot, I know. If you had told me all I know you could, I never should have cared for you again! It's pretty damnable, that, isn't it? But swine like me go on repenting and repenting, and then we're twice as bad again. We're cursed, I think; we— —"

She put her hand over his mouth. "It's over now," she said: "time up," and laughed, herself again.

He looked at her as at some miracle beyond his understanding. "And you won't ever long to—well, to be Zoë again?"

She looked him full in the face, and her eyes smiled happiness. "No," she said, "I've found myself out as well. I'm nothing but a woman after all!"

"The dearest woman in the whole world," he replied and kissed her.

Ruth knocked at the door.